TANGLED VOWS

ANNA STONE

© 2020 Anna Stone

All rights reserved. No part of this publication may be replicated, reproduced, or redistributed in any form without the prior written consent of the publisher.

This is a work of fiction. Names, characters, places, and incidents either are the products of the author's imagination or are used fictitiously. Any resemblance to actual persons, living or dead, businesses, companies, events, or locales is entirely coincidental.

Cover by Kasmit Covers

ISBN: 9780648419266

CHAPTER 1

Ruby entered the hotel bar. It was past 2 a.m., but as usual, the room was buzzing. The excitement never stopped on the Vegas strip.

She took a seat at a table midway between the bar and the entrance, the perfect spot for people-watching.

And the perfect spot for people to see Ruby.

A waitress came by to take her order. As Ruby waited for her drink to arrive, she crossed her legs and leaned back, surveying the room. The hotel was one of the most exclusive venues on the strip, not to mention one of the most expensive. The guests were of the highest caliber, all wealthy, upper-class, with discerning tastes.

It was the ideal place for Ruby to find clients. And she needed clients. She'd been out of the escort game for far too long, having given it up after entering a long-term arrangement with a client. When the arrangement had ended, Ruby had taken up a job as a waitress, but she'd quit after a few weeks so she could return to escorting.

However, getting back on the horse was proving difficult. Although she'd had plenty of interest, Ruby was struggling to find anyone she wanted to take on as a client. It should have been easy. In the past, she'd been able to pick and choose her clients as she pleased. Ruby wasn't just any escort. Only the wealthiest could afford even a minute of her time. It was how she'd been able to make a living without needing to hustle. At least, until now.

Ruby needed to start making money soon. She was behind on rent. Her credit cards were maxed out. She was broke.

The waitress returned with her drink. Ruby sipped it slowly as she watched the crowd. What had changed? Was she losing her touch? She'd always been good at her job. She knew exactly what her clients wanted. They wanted the experience of having a young, beautiful woman at their beck and call for everything from dinner to far more intimate activities. They wanted a whole experience, and Ruby delivered just that.

And she knew how to attract the right kind of clientele. Her dress and shoes were designer, the jewelry she wore expensive but understated. She'd scrimped and saved for her outfits or had received them from former clients as gifts, all so she'd look the part. Her dark blonde hair was styled to perfection, and she'd learned to carry herself with sophistication and class, all to mark her as an escort of a special kind.

It was all an illusion, of course. Even before she'd taken a break from escorting, Ruby's life had been far from glamorous. She spent most of her time lounging around her crappy one-bedroom apartment in sweats. The effortless confidence and charm she projected for her clients? Also an illusion. She was a mess of anxieties and unpaid bills.

Ruby sighed. Why was she finding this so difficult? Could it be that the problem was Ruby herself? Could it be that her heart just wasn't in it anymore? It would be understandable, considering everything that had happened with her last client. Over time, that person had become far more than just a client.

And then he'd shattered her, along with her life.

Since then, Ruby had been trying her hardest to pick up the pieces, to rebuild her life, herself, again. But after being powerless for so long, she didn't even know where to start.

Ruby sat up straighter. She wasn't going to let that get to her. She was going to get back into the game.

She stirred her drink, a martini, continuing to scan the room. As she did, she noticed a woman walk through the door.

Ruby watched the woman surreptitiously. She had long brown hair, one shade away from black, and dark, bewitching eyes. Her elegant black off the shoulder dress was form-fitting, but in a tasteful way. She was on the shorter side, but her confident bearing, the purposeful way she walked, made her presence feel far more imposing. Several heads turned as she walked past, but the woman paid them no mind. She simply sat down at the bar and ordered a drink.

Ruby took another sip of her martini. If she'd learned one thing, it was that the kind of women who employed her services—rich, powerful, confident in their sexuality—had extremely specific desires. Some of them were exactly the same in bed as they were in all other parts of their lives, commanding and in control. Others were the complete opposite, seeking refuge in Ruby from their demanding lives, wanting to let go and hand Ruby the reins.

She knew which type she preferred. Which kind of woman was this dark-haired goddess?

Ruby was getting ahead of herself. Was this woman even interested in women? Was she looking for company?

Ruby studied her, searching for answers. The bartender set the woman's order in front of her, a bottle of top-shelf scotch and a single glass. That was a good sign. For starters, it meant that the woman was wealthy enough to afford Ruby's time. More importantly, it suggested she wanted to drink her troubles away. In Ruby's experience, people in that situation wanted company just as much as they wanted to drink.

Providing company was the main part of Ruby's job. Her more intimate services? Anyone could provide that. But the company of a beautiful, glamorous woman who would listen to their every word was something much harder to come by. It wasn't unusual for her clients to bare their hearts to her, their deepest desires and darkest secrets exposed between the sheets.

What secrets was this woman hiding? What desires did she harbor?

Suddenly, the woman looked in Ruby's direction. Her gaze fell upon Ruby, sweeping over her body before returning to her eyes. Ruby's pulse quickened. The woman's stare wasn't greedy or lustful, like the leers so many of Ruby's potential clients gave her. The look in the woman's eyes spoke of desire that was more than physical. It was as if she were trying to see deeper into Ruby.

One thing was certain. The woman wanted her in a way that Ruby didn't quite understand.

Ruby held the woman's gaze, ignoring her racing heart. She'd played this game enough times to know what would happen next. In just a few moments, the woman would come over and speak to her.

But instead, the woman turned back to stare at her drink.

Ruby recrossed her legs and let her eyes wander around the room. So the woman needed a little convincing. That wouldn't be too hard. Ruby would wait until the woman glanced in her direction again, and then she'd give the woman a flirtatious, inviting smile. Then the woman would walk right over to Ruby and snap her up, thinking it was her idea all along. That was how it worked.

But as the minutes passed, the woman didn't look Ruby's way again. Nor did she do anything else. She simply continued to stare at her drink.

Ruby frowned. Perhaps the woman needed a little encouragement. Ruby liked to let clients approach her, but this was a special case. Ruby needed a client, and this woman intrigued her. The woman was interested in her too, but it was clear that she wasn't going to make the first move. Ruby would have to do so herself.

So why did the thought of approaching the woman make her chest flutter? It was dangerous, the effect the woman was having on Ruby. When it came to her job, letting feelings get involved made it all too easy for her to get hurt. She'd learned her lesson from her last client. Ruby needed to keep her head.

She steeled herself. The woman was just another potential client.

Ruby picked up her drink and headed to the bar.

Yvonne stared at the bottle of scotch before her. She'd come to the bar after making an exit from her friend's bachelorette party. She'd originally planned to turn in for the night, but she'd found herself with too much on her mind. Drinking her troubles away instead wasn't the smartest idea, especially considering how much she'd already drunk over the weekend. She was usually far more responsible.

But tonight, she had a good reason to drink.

Yvonne picked up the bottle and poured a few fingers of scotch into her glass. She stared down at it as she swirled it around. Millions of dollars. Her inheritance.

And it was about to slip through her fingers.

"That's a lot of scotch for one person."

Yvonne turned toward the voice. Standing beside her was a tall, slender woman with long, blonde hair, dark as old gold. She wore a stylish red dress and black pumps. Her eyes were a pale blue and her lips were the same inviting shade of crimson as her dress. Yvonne had noticed the woman earlier. It was impossible not to notice someone like her.

But Yvonne wasn't interested in company right now. Without acknowledging the woman, she turned back to her drink and took a long sip.

The woman sat down in the chair next to Yvonne, a martini glass in her hand. "Don't worry, I have a drink of my own. I just thought you could use some company. I'm Ruby, by the way."

Yvonne put down her glass and looked at Ruby again. Ruby smiled. Her red lips were so alluring, her teasing eyes seeming to beg for Yvonne's attention.

Yvonne held back a sigh. Clearly, she had too much on her mind, because it had taken her far too long to realize what was going on.

"I don't do escorts," she said.

"What makes you think I'm an escort?" Ruby asked.

"It isn't often that women approach me at bars. Or at all." Yvonne was well aware that she gave off an intimidating air. It was an advantage. It kept people away. *Most* people.

Ruby flicked her long hair over her shoulders. "Maybe I'm the only one who's game enough."

"Actually, I prefer it that way."

"Oh? So you're the type who likes to do the chasing? I prefer that in a woman too." Ruby peered at Yvonne from under hooded eyes. "You're exactly my type."

Yvonne gave Ruby a hard stare. "You say that, yet you came over here, dangling yourself before me like bait. I can see right through this act of yours."

Ruby's cheeks turned scarlet, and she lowered her gaze. It seemed she wasn't used to being called out on her games. Yvonne felt a pang of satisfaction.

But Ruby quickly regained her composure. "What act? I got tired of waiting for you to come to me, that's all." She looked back up at Yvonne, her honeyed voice dropping low. "And now that I'm here, I'm all yours."

Desire flickered along Yvonne's skin. That coy manner of Ruby's might be an act, but she couldn't fake the way her skin had reddened when Yvonne had given her that stern look...

No. Ruby was an escort. It was her job to be whoever her client wanted her to be. And although Yvonne had a weakness for women who liked to please her, she had no interest in a woman who wanted to please her for money. Yvonne wanted a woman whose need to serve ran far deeper. She doubted that Ruby genuinely harbored such desires.

"You're wasting your time," Yvonne said. "I don't do escorts."

"Well," Ruby said. "It's been a quiet night for me. And it's getting late, so I'm not going to find any clients tonight. I'm going to call it a night right after I finish this drink. So how about we chat until then?"

Yvonne raised an eyebrow. So Ruby was dropping the pretense of not being an escort? It was obviously just a change in tactics, another attempt to make Yvonne drop her guard. But Yvonne wasn't going to fall for Ruby's tricks. She didn't like being toyed with.

But she did enjoy making Ruby squirm.

"All right," Yvonne said. "Let's chat."

Ruby draped an arm on the bar next to her. "So, what brings you to Vegas?"

"A friend of mine is getting married. We're here for the bachelorette weekend."

"Sounds like fun."

"Perhaps if you're easily entertained." Vegas wasn't Yvonne's idea of a good time, but Yvonne was maid of honor, so she'd had no choice but to come along. Between that, and the constant reminders of all things marriage, she'd been in a bad mood the entire weekend.

It must have shown on Yvonne's face. "You seem preoccupied," Ruby said. "Something on your mind?"

Yvonne scoffed. "What's on my mind is above your pay grade."

"You'd be surprised. People talk to me about their problems a lot. It comes with the territory."

"You're admitting you're an escort?"

"Maybe I'm a therapist." Ruby stirred her drink with the toothpick, swirling the olives around in it. "So what is it? Is it about a woman?"

"What makes you think I'm into women?"

Ruby shrugged. "It's just a feeling. So you *are* into women?"

Yvonne fixed her eyes on Ruby's. "Are you?"

There it was again, that faint flush that rose up Ruby's cheeks at Yvonne's words. Yvonne held back a smile. She had Ruby wrapped around her finger.

But Ruby's confident facade quickly returned. "I wouldn't be over here if I wasn't. So, what's this problem of yours?"

Yvonne folded her arms across her chest, scrutinizing Ruby. Was it reckless telling a stranger, an escort she met at a bar, about her inheritance? Probably. However, she doubted that this woman was capable of scamming her. Yvonne wasn't easily manipulated. She was one of the most successful businesswomen in the country, with a reputation for being ruthless and unyielding. Despite Ruby's attempts to seduce her, it was clear that Yvonne had the upper hand.

"All right," she said. "Here's the short version. When my father died, he left me an inheritance. But it came with conditions. In order to gain access to it, I need to get married within ten years of his death."

Yvonne's father had never liked that she was a lesbian. He hadn't liked a lot about his daughter, but that was one major sticking point. He'd obviously hoped that the terms of the inheritance would sway her into a relationship with a man, but he hadn't specified the gender of who Yvonne needed to marry. Her father had been so old-fashioned that the possibility of same-sex marriage being legalized had never occurred to him.

But that had been no help to Yvonne. She wasn't the relationship, let alone the marrying, type.

"It's been almost ten years since my father died," Yvonne said. "And here I am, unmarried, which means all that money is going to go to my half-brother instead." It was bad enough that Nicholas had already inherited most of Yvonne's father's fortune. Now, he was going to get the rest of it.

"Huh." Ruby took the toothpick from her drink and slid it into her mouth, sucking the olives from it. "So there's really no way around the whole marriage thing? No loopholes?"

"If there was, I would have found it." Yvonne picked up her scotch and swallowed a mouthful. "I've already accepted it. The money is as good as gone." She'd resigned herself to that fact already, although she wasn't happy about it.

Silence fell between them. Yvonne wasn't surprised that Ruby had nothing to say about her problem. However, Yvonne had to admit, she was intrigued by the woman, though she had no intention of employing Ruby's services. She didn't sleep with escorts.

But there was no harm in enjoying Ruby's company for a little while longer.

Ruby took one last sip of her cocktail, emptying her glass. "Well, that's my drink done." She stood up. "It was good talking to you."

She glanced at Yvonne, a hint of disappointment in her eyes. When Yvonne said nothing, she turned and began walking away.

"Stop," Yvonne commanded.

Ruby halted, turning back to Yvonne.

Yvonne beckoned her with a finger. "Do you drink scotch?"

Ruby nodded.

"You were right. This is too much scotch for one person. Why don't you help me with it?"

Ruby's lips parted slightly. She gave Yvonne a tantalizing smile. "Like I said, I'm all yours."

For a split second, Yvonne wondered if this was a bad idea. Getting drunk with an escort in Vegas? That was irresponsible.

She pushed the thought aside and caught the eye of the bartender. He came over to them.

"We need another glass," Yvonne said.

CHAPTER 2

Ruby awoke with a blistering headache. It was like someone had taken a jackhammer to her skull. As she rolled over, a wave of nausea hit her.

She groaned. She hadn't had a hangover this bad since she was nineteen.

Ruby lay there with her eyes closed, waiting for the world to stop spinning. She definitely wasn't in her own bed. The sheets enveloping her were too soft, the mattress too springy. Whose bed was she in? A client's? She could barely remember a thing.

Ruby opened her eyes, immediately raising a hand to shield them from the harsh sunlight streaming through the window. It appeared to be late morning. She looked around the room. It was one of the premium suites at the hotel of the bar she'd been at the night before. She'd only been in a suite like this once. Only the real high rollers could afford them, which made them out of reach for most people, even her usual clients.

She glanced at the bed next to her. She was alone. At the

very least, she remembered who she'd been expecting to find—the woman from the bar. She racked her brains for a name. *Yvonne.* After meeting at the bar, she and Yvonne had made their best effort to finish the bottle of scotch. Everything after that was a blur. Did they have sex? That was unlikely, considering Yvonne's insistence that she didn't 'do' escorts. And Ruby never mixed large quantities of alcohol with sex.

So why did she have the feeling she'd done something reckless?

Ruby brushed her hair out of her face. As she did, she felt the metal of a ring graze her skin. That was odd. She didn't normally wear rings. Still half asleep, she brought her hand up before her face. Her left hand.

On her ring finger was a gold band.

Oh no.

Ruby sat bolt upright. Bad idea. A wave of nausea came over her, but this time it didn't pass. She scrambled out of bed, her legs tangling in the sheets, and made a beeline for the nearby bathroom. She shut the door behind her and fell to her knees in front of the toilet, just in time for the contents of her stomach to come back up.

Once she was sure her stomach was empty, Ruby flushed the toilet and went over to the sink, her head still spinning. As she rinsed out her mouth, she heard a knock on the bathroom door.

"Ruby?"

She froze. She knew the voice from the night before. *Yvonne.* Ruby braced herself on the vanity countertop as dizziness overcame her again.

Yvonne called her name again. "Are you in there?"

"Yes," Ruby croaked. "I'll be out in a minute."

Ruby listened to Yvonne's footsteps recede from the door as the world righted itself again. What the hell had happened the night before? She recalled their conversation at the bar. Yvonne had told Ruby that she had an inheritance she couldn't claim unless she was married. And now Ruby was in the bathroom of Yvonne's suite, wearing a wedding ring.

No. No way.

Ruby took a few deep breaths. She needed to find out what was going on. She splashed some cold water on her face and looked at it in the mirror. She was a mess, her hair in disarray and her eyes puffy.

Why was she even thinking about how she looked? She had far bigger problems.

Ruby took another deep breath and opened the bathroom door to find Yvonne sitting on the edge of the bed. She looked just as mesmerizing as she had the night before. Once again, she was dressed in a black dress, a simpler one this time. Her dark hair was pulled back into a bun, her hazel eyes greener in the daylight. Her arms were crossed, and she studied Ruby with narrowed eyes, her expression inscrutable.

Ruby's eyes flicked down to Yvonne's left hand. Sure enough, she wore a gold wedding band that matched Ruby's. Ruby's stomach flipped. For a moment, she thought she was going to throw up again.

"Ruby." Yvonne gestured to a chair in the corner. "Why don't you have a seat?"

"I'll stand." She might have to run to the bathroom again.

Silence hung between them. Yvonne continued to study

Ruby, her demeanor calm and inscrutable. Why wasn't she freaking out about the situation like Ruby was?

Finally, Yvonne spoke. "You don't remember last night, do you?"

Ruby shook her head. "Not a thing."

"That makes two of us."

Ruby frowned. If Yvonne didn't remember anything, why was she so calm? She didn't seem at all flustered by the fact that she was now married to a stranger. What was going on?

"The last thing I remember is pouring us both another round of scotch," Yvonne said. "Then I woke up to find a ring on my finger and you in my bed. I found this on the table." She held up a piece of paper. It was a marriage certificate with both their names on it. "Apparently, we thought this was a good solution to my inheritance issue."

Fractured snippets of the night came back to Ruby. They'd left the hotel bar, to go god knew where. They'd drunk some more. Eventually, they'd ended up in a little 'chapel' standing before a celebrant dressed as Elvis. Ruby didn't remember anything in between, like when and why they'd decided to get married.

Ruby shook her head. "We need to undo this."

"If that's what you want," Yvonne said. "We can get an annulment on the basis that we were unable to consent to the marriage because of our inebriated states. We fill out some forms, and it will be like this never happened."

Ruby breathed a sigh of relief.

"Of course, there's another option."

Ruby froze. "What do you mean?"

"We can take advantage of the situation. We can remain married. Come to some kind of agreement."

"You want to stay married?"

"Only until I can get my inheritance. Of course, I'll make it worth your while."

Ruby shook her head. It was a crazy idea. Besides, Ruby knew better than to get into an arrangement with a client, especially after the last time she'd done so.

Nothing could possibly make this worthwhile. Right?

"*How* would you make it worth my while?" Ruby asked.

"It's simple. Once I get the inheritance, you get a share of the money," Yvonne said. "How does one million sound?"

Ruby's eyes widened. "A million dollars?"

"Of course, there are additional perks to being my wife. I'm sure a woman like you is accustomed to luxury, but the luxury I can provide you with goes beyond the gaudy glitz of Vegas." She waved her hand around the room. "You'll have everything you could possibly want."

Ruby twisted the ring around her finger absently. That did sound tempting.

"One of the conditions of the inheritance is that I need to stay married for a year in order to get the full amount. But once the year is up and the money is in my hands, you'll get your share, and we can get a divorce and go our separate ways."

A year. That was a long time. But one million dollars was so much money. There were so many things Ruby could do with it. If she was smart, she could set herself up for life.

"What do you want in exchange?" she asked

"For you to be my wife," Yvonne replied. "At least, to

outside eyes. In order to claim my inheritance, I need to have a witness to the fact that our relationship is genuine, so we'll need to convince the world that we're a real married couple. You'll come live with me, in my apartment. For the majority of the time, you'll be free to do as you please. Your life will be your own." Yvonne crossed one slender leg over the other. "But when I need you by my side, as my wife, you'll be mine."

A thrill whispered through Ruby's body. "I don't know."

"I'd give you time to decide, but unfortunately, time isn't something I have to spare right now. I fly out of Vegas tonight. You have until 4 p.m. this afternoon to think about it."

It was already almost midday. That wasn't enough time to make such a big decision.

Wait, am I seriously considering this?

"In the meantime," Yvonne continued. "I'll fill out the annulment paperwork. If you decide you want to go through with the annulment, I'll submit it. But if you want to take up my offer, we'll remain married, and you'll fly home with me."

Ruby nodded. She was so overwhelmed that it was all she could do.

Yvonne rose from the bed, smoothing down her dress. "I have to go meet my friends for lunch. Keep the room for the rest of the day. Order room service, do whatever you like." Yvonne locked her gaze on Ruby. "Consider it a taste of what lies ahead if you agree to our arrangement."

Ruby's breath caught in her chest. Yvonne's look had that effect on her. And it made her want to say yes.

"I'll see you this afternoon, at the bar where we met," Yvonne said. "You do remember where we met, don't you?"

Ruby nodded.

"Good." Yvonne paused. "For the record, I spent the night on the couch. We did *not* sleep together."

With that, she turned and left the room.

Ruby wandered over to the bed in a daze and lay down. Her head was swimming from both the hangover and Yvonne's offer. One million dollars? A year, married to a stranger, and an incredibly sexy one at that?

She glanced at the ring on her finger. Why was she hesitating? She desperately needed the money. Her credit cards were maxed out, and it was only a matter of time before she went home to find an eviction notice on her door. It should have been a no-brainer. She'd done jobs like this before, jobs that were long-term and exclusive. But the last time she'd done that kind of gig, her client had turned into something more. They'd started a relationship.

And that relationship had shattered her.

Ruby shook herself. This wasn't like the last time. This time, it would be a business transaction only, with no feelings involved. Ruby definitely wasn't going to let feelings get involved. Although she was wildly attracted to Yvonne, that was just on a physical level. Ruby found Yvonne's presence irresistible, but it was nothing more than that.

She looked around the room. One million dollars would probably make things worth her while. Judging by the lavish suite Ruby was in, as well as the way Yvonne dressed, the woman was seriously loaded. Was one million dollars even worth anything to her?

Ruby picked up the marriage certificate from the nightstand where Yvonne had left it. It had both of their full, legal names on it. *Ruth Josephine Scott. Yvonne Lin Maxwell.*

Ruby frowned. Why did that name sound familiar? Ignoring her hangover-induced nausea, she got up from the bed and located her purse. She pulled out her phone and typed Yvonne's name into a search.

As she read the results, everything started to fall into place. A smile tugged at Ruby's lips. She was no more certain of whether she wanted to accept Yvonne's offer or not.

But if she was going to do this, she had to make sure Yvonne really made it worth her while.

CHAPTER 3

Yvonne sat at the bar, nursing a cup of coffee. She was tempted to order something stronger, but after the previous night, she'd learned her lesson.

Yvonne hadn't been lying when she'd said she didn't remember the events of the previous night. She'd never do anything as rash as marrying a stranger while sober. When she'd woken up, she'd wondered if Ruby had conned her somehow, seducing Yvonne into a marriage in order to steal her fortune. That was, until Ruby had come out of the bathroom, clearly just as surprised about the situation as Yvonne.

It was a crazy situation. But now that the opportunity had presented itself, Yvonne wasn't going to let it slip away.

She checked the time. It was just past 4 p.m. Ruby would be here any minute. Yvonne had brought the required forms for the annulment, but she doubted she'd need them. She was certain that Ruby would say yes. Although Ruby had appeared unsure earlier, something had sparked behind her blue eyes when Yvonne had mentioned the money.

And the same thing had happened when Yvonne had said that Ruby would be *hers*.

Did the idea appeal to Ruby? It certainly appealed to Yvonne. Although she had no intention of their arrangement being anything but business, she couldn't deny that she was attracted to Ruby. Was there a chance that Ruby was the type of woman she pretended to be?

Did Ruby truly have a submissive side?

It didn't matter. This was purely a financial agreement. A transaction. It could never be anything more. Yvonne needed to focus on the reason she was doing this—to get her inheritance.

Although Yvonne didn't need the money, she wanted it, for good reasons. Not to mention, she hated the idea of her half-brother getting what was rightfully hers. Nicholas had already stolen all her father's love and attention growing up, and now he was going to get this too, on top of all the money her father had left him. And her brother was, quite simply, an asshole. He'd made Yvonne's life hell growing up.

She finished off her coffee. As she did, Ruby walked through the door.

Yvonne couldn't help but stare. Ruby had cleaned up since the morning and was looking just as captivating as the night before. She sauntered over to Yvonne and slid into the seat next to her.

"You look like you've come to a decision," Yvonne said.

Ruby smiled slightly. "Not quite."

Yvonne stifled a frown. "You haven't decided yet?"

Ruby caught the eye of the bartender and ordered a drink, taking her time. Yvonne narrowed her eyes. What was the woman playing at?

Finally, Ruby turned back to Yvonne. "I'm not going to lie. Your offer is very tempting. But I'm just not sure it's worth my while."

Yvonne raised an eyebrow. "Are you trying to negotiate with me?"

"I'm just saying, I think you need me more than I need you."

Yvonne pushed her irritation aside. Apparently, she'd underestimated Ruby. "What do you want? More money?"

"We both know that a million dollars is nothing to you." Ruby crossed her arms. "I know who you are, *Yvonne Maxwell*. You own Mistress Media."

So Ruby had looked Yvonne up. That explained it. "I don't own it outright. I'm one of the owners. There are five of us."

"The details aren't important. What's important is that you own a stake in one of the biggest media empires in the world. You're worth millions. Billions, even."

What Ruby was saying was true, but all Yvonne's money meant nothing when she couldn't access it, like right now. It was why she wanted her inheritance in the first place. Once it was in her hands, all her money troubles would disappear.

Yvonne folded her arms across her chest. "How much?"

"Ten million," Ruby said.

Yvonne scoffed. "I don't think so." Ruby had guts, to say the least. Yvonne didn't know whether it made her like Ruby more or less. Unfortunately for Ruby, negotiating was what Yvonne did for a living.

"Fine. Eight million."

"Perhaps I wasn't clear," Yvonne said calmly. "You'll be living with me, in my apartment, with every expense paid for, for an entire year. And not just the basics. *Everything.* Clothes, shoes, jewelry. Expensive dinners. Luxury cars taking you wherever you want to go. Or even a car of your own, if you'd like." Yvonne locked her gaze on Ruby's. "You'll be my wife, after all. If you're going to play the part, I'm going to give you everything you need to make it so. You'll have everything you could ever want. Everything you've ever desired."

For a moment, the determination in Ruby's eyes was overshadowed by lust. Was it lust for a life of luxury? Or lust for something else?

Someone, perhaps?

Ruby pressed her lips into a line, her resolve returning. "What I desire is eight million dollars."

"Two million," Yvonne said firmly. "And you'll get your own credit card to spend as you please. Within reasonable limits, of course."

"I'm not going any lower. A whole year of my life is a long time to give up, even if I'll be living it in luxury."

Ruby was right. If Yvonne was going to exploit someone, she might as well compensate her fairly. And what was a few million in the grand scheme of things? If Yvonne played her cards right, she'd have millions at her disposal soon enough. And that wasn't counting the billions she already held in assets.

"Five million." Yvonne held up her hand, forestalling Ruby's reply. "And I'll sweeten the deal. The fine print of my inheritance states that I get half of it after being married for three months, and the other half after a year. I'll make you the same deal. You get two and a half million at the three-month mark. Make it to a year, and you'll get the rest."

Ruby hesitated.

Yvonne had her. "Five million. That's my final offer." She didn't give Ruby a chance to speak. "And in exchange, I expect you to play the part of my wife to *perfection*." Yvonne leaned in closer to her. "You will be my wife in every sense of the word."

This time, the lust that flashed behind Ruby's eyes lasted long enough for Yvonne to know she hadn't imagined it. And this time, it was no clearer whether it was about the money or Yvonne herself.

Yvonne sat back. "To the outside world, that is."

Ruby glanced away, chewing her lip in thought. Yvonne waited in silence. She already knew Ruby's answer. She already knew she had Ruby hooked.

And she couldn't deny the satisfaction it gave her.

Finally, Ruby spoke. "Five million dollars. Half at three months, half after a year. I'll be your wife. I'll be more than your wife." Her voice fell to a sultry whisper. "I'll be whatever you want me to be."

Yvonne ignored the twinge of desire she felt at Ruby's words. "Just so we're clear, I don't want anything from you except for you to act as my wife in public. That's *all*. This is purely a business arrangement."

"Sure, I hear you." But Ruby's smile suggested otherwise.

Was that going to be a problem? Yvonne hoped not, because she didn't have any other options.

"We have a deal." Just to drive home the point, Yvonne held out her hand for Ruby to shake.

But when Ruby slipped her hand into Yvonne's, it had the opposite effect. Her soft touch was electrifying.

Yvonne broke off the handshake. "I was planning to fly

out in a couple of hours, but we'll catch a red-eye later tonight instead. That will give you time to pack. Only the essentials, of course. I'll buy you everything you need when we get back home."

Ruby nodded, her face suddenly filled with uncertainty. Was it just now dawning on her what she'd agreed to? Yvonne didn't have time to deal with whatever Ruby was going through. She had business to take care of.

She finished off her coffee. "I need to let my friends know I won't be flying back with them." She'd break the news of her marriage to them first thing in the morning at work on Monday. "After that, I'll be in my suite. Come find me if you have any questions."

Ruby nodded.

Yvonne left the bar. The deal was done. At the end of the year, Yvonne would have her inheritance. Ruby would have her five million dollars. They would go their separate ways.

All they had to do between now and then was convince the world that their marriage was real.

CHAPTER 4

Ruby stepped through the front door of Yvonne's apartment and looked around. The apartment was huge, and it made the Vegas suite look tacky and cheap. Although it was uncluttered and plainly decorated, it didn't feel empty. All the decor had a clean, minimalistic richness.

"This is a nice place." Was this really Ruby's home for an entire year? She could get used to this.

"I've only lived here a couple of years," Yvonne said. "The penthouse was taken, so I had to settle."

Yvonne tipped the doorman for bringing their bags up and headed into the apartment. Ruby followed, carefully containing the awe she felt. She didn't want to look too impressed. That was a turn-off.

Not that it mattered in this case. Yvonne had made herself very clear that their arrangement was purely business, and they were already locked into it by the rings on their fingers. Ruby didn't have to seduce Yvonne, didn't have to play the perfect girlfriend. She didn't have to pretend to be Yvonne's fantasy. But Ruby had become so used to turning herself into the kind of person her client wanted her to be.

Ruby examined Yvonne as she followed her. Was 'wife' really all that Yvonne wanted Ruby to be?

Yvonne led her down a hall. "I have to be at work in an hour, so I'll make this quick. You can have this room." She opened a door to the right. "The housekeeper is due in today; I'll have her make it up for you."

Yvonne was giving Ruby her own bedroom? Clearly, she was serious about keeping their arrangement platonic. Ruby peered through the door to find a huge bedroom with a king-sized bed and an adjoining bathroom, along with a large sunny window through which the city below them could be seen.

"You're welcome to replace the furnishings and decor to suit your tastes," Yvonne said. "On that topic, I have something for you. Wait here."

Ruby waited in the hall while Yvonne disappeared into another room. When she returned, she was holding a card in her hand.

"Here." Yvonne handed Ruby the card. It was a credit card bearing Yvonne's name. "This is yours. Use it to buy anything you need. If you're going to live here for a year, I want you to be comfortable. Buy yourself a new wardrobe. You'll need some pieces for when you accompany me on special occasions, but I'll take care of those. The basics are up to you. Just make sure any outfits you buy are befitting of your status as my wife. That shouldn't be difficult for you." Her eyes swept down Ruby's body. "I can tell you're a woman of excellent tastes."

Ruby bit her lip. Yvonne's probing gaze made her skin hot.

"Don't go too crazy," Yvonne said. "If you want something big like a car, ask me first."

Ruby nodded. With all these demands, she couldn't help but feel like Yvonne was treating her like a child rather than her wife. However, something told Ruby that Yvonne would treat her actual wife the exact same way.

"I need a shower before work, so I'll leave you to settle in. Have a look around. Make yourself at home. You're free to do whatever you want during the day, but I need you home tonight. We need to discuss our cover story."

Ruby nodded again. They'd talked about coming up with a cover story when they'd gotten on the plane in Vegas, but they'd been too tired to do anything but sleep during the red-eye flight. It had been Ruby's first time flying first class and she'd slept through everything.

"We'll also need to make this arrangement of ours official," Yvonne said. "I'll draw up a contract. Usually, I'd have my lawyers do it, but we should keep that part of our arrangement between us, for obvious reasons. I think both of us would feel more secure with our agreement in writing."

"That's a good idea," Ruby said.

"I'll leave you to it. Let me know if you need anything." Yvonne headed to the end of the hall to what was presumably the master bedroom.

Ruby entered her bedroom and sat on the bed. Distantly, she heard the sound of running water as Yvonne turned on the shower. She looked around her. This was her life now.

She'd packed her bags and left her old life behind overnight. But she'd had very little to leave behind in the first place.

And it was all because of *him*, her last client. Because of him, Ruby had lost everything. She had no friends, having drifted apart from them all while trapped in a toxic relationship. She hadn't spoken to her family in a long time either. She still had some loose ends to deal with, like her apartment and all her things, but that was all.

Her old life was well and truly behind her. *He* was well and truly behind her. She had all Yvonne's money at her disposal. She had all the spare time she could possibly want. She had the opportunity to repair all the damage he'd done, to rebuild her life again.

The only problem was, she had no idea how to do that.

Yvonne rode the elevator up to the Mistress Media offices. As usual, she was one of the first people there. Soon, the sprawling top floor office would be swarming with activity.

Mistress Media was the vision of Madison Sloane, the company's CEO and Yvonne's closest friend. Madison had started Mistress years ago, and in the space of less than a decade, the female-led media company had grown from a single publication to an international empire.

Yvonne had been there from the beginning. She was the COO of Mistress, and Madison's right-hand woman. From a business perspective, Yvonne essentially ran the company. She had better business sense than Madison, a former journalist, so Madison deferred to her in that department. Generally, Yvonne didn't work well with others, but herself,

Madison, and the three others who ran Mistress made an excellent team.

Yvonne reached her office and sat down at her desk, settling in. She had several emails to send, and only half an hour before the Monday morning meeting started. She and the four other women who made up the Mistress executive team held a meeting every Monday morning so they could catch up on everything, business and personal. They were a tight-knit group, most of whom had been friends long before they'd started Mistress Media together.

By the time Yvonne finished with the most urgent of her emails, it was almost time for the meeting to begin. She headed to the conference room. Through the glass walls, she spotted a slender brunette sitting at the head of the table. Of course Madison was the only one of them who was already there. This was despite the fact that it had been Madison's bachelorette party they'd been in Vegas for over the weekend. Madison had still shown up at work on time and looking none the worse for wear.

Yvonne opened the door and strode inside.

Madison gave her a nod. "Good morning."

"Madison." Yvonne sat down at the table. "Recovered from the weekend already, I take it?"

"I'm fine. I didn't go as crazy as the rest of you."

"Speaking of the rest of us, where are the others?"

"I saw Lydia earlier," Madison said. "She should be here soon. I'm assuming Gabrielle and Amber are still recovering, but I'm sure they'll turn up. By the way, did you take care of whatever it was you needed to do in Vegas?"

"More or less." Yvonne had told the others that she needed to stay back in Vegas to take care of something.

She'd needed time to work out how to break the news of her 'marriage' to her friends. However, she still hadn't come up with a way to do so.

"What exactly did you need to take care of?" Madison asked.

Yvonne folded her hands in front of her on the table, stalling for time. She didn't realize her mistake until Madison's eyes fell to Yvonne's hands.

Madison tilted her head to the side. "Is that... a wedding ring?"

Yvonne rearranged her hands. "Yes."

"And why are you wearing a wedding ring?"

"Because I'm married."

"What? Since when? And to who?" Realization dawned on Madison's face. "Did you get married in Vegas? Is that why you stayed behind?"

"Yes," Yvonne said.

"Yes? That's all? Aren't you going to explain yourself?"

"What is there to explain? I got married to a woman in Vegas. Her name is Ruby."

"And?"

Yvonne gritted her teeth. "It's a long story."

Madison frowned. "Yvonne, what's going on? Is everything all right with you? Are you having some kind of crisis?"

"Christ, Madison, you think it's more likely that I'm going crazy than that I genuinely got married?"

"You have to admit, this is completely out of character for you. And you seemed a little off while we were in Vegas."

"I assure you, I'm not having some kind of breakdown." Yvonne paused. She'd been planning to maintain the marriage ruse with everyone, including Madison. She didn't like the idea of lying to her friends, but the ends justified the means. She needed the world to believe her marriage to Ruby was real.

But as she faced her closest friend, Yvonne found she just couldn't lie.

"Look, if I tell you the truth, you can't tell anyone else," Yvonne said.

"Yvonne, we've known each other since we were teenagers," Madison said. "You know you can trust me."

"Then promise me that you won't tell anyone, no matter what."

"All right. I won't tell a soul."

Yvonne gathered her thoughts. "When my father died, he left me an inheritance."

"He did? You've never mentioned it before."

"Because I was never able to claim it. It came with strings. The biggest one being, I need to be married within ten years of my father's death in order to claim it, otherwise it all goes to Nicholas. It's been almost ten years since he died."

"That's why you got married?" Madison asked. "For the money?"

Yvonne nodded.

"Are you having financial problems? You know you could have asked me for help. I can lend you something. Or you could ask Amber if you need something more substantial. She'd help you out in a heartbeat."

Yvonne shook her head. It had occurred to her to ask one of her friends for a loan, but she hated asking anyone for help. "I don't *need* the money. I could really use it, that's all. At the moment, all my money is tied up. I have my eye on some investments. I simply need some capital for it."

The truth was, her current financial situation wasn't great. She'd made some risky investments in the past year that hadn't panned out as she'd predicted. She was far from bankrupt, and she had plenty of money invested, but they were the kind of investments that paid off in the long term and couldn't simply be withdrawn on a whim. She didn't have much liquid capital right now.

Which wouldn't have been a problem if she only had herself to worry about.

Madison raised an eyebrow. "You decided to marry a woman you met in Vegas for money for investments?"

"The marriage is only temporary," Yvonne said. "We only need to stay married for a year for me to get the money. It's not a big deal. It isn't like I'm going to get married for real any time soon." Yvonne didn't have room in her life for romance. "Ruby is on the same page about our arrangement. It's purely business. She pretends to be my wife for a year, I give her a small part of my inheritance. It's the perfect solution to my problem."

Madison scoffed. "It's also the craziest solution."

Yvonne held up her hands. "It's already done, Madison. And now that I've told you, you can't tell anyone else. The conditions of my inheritance are clear—my marriage must be genuine for me to be able to claim the money. No one can know that our marriage is a sham."

"You want me to lie for you?"

"Of course not." Yvonne would need to find a witness to attest to the authenticity of marriage to Ruby, but she couldn't ask Madison to do it. She'd find someone else. "All

I'm asking is that you keep this to yourself. Madison, you know I wouldn't ask if this wasn't important."

"You're right." Madison sighed. "I won't say anything. But this is so extreme. Are you sure you're not in any trouble?"

"I'm fine." Yvonne paused. "The truth is, this isn't just about investments. I want to use some of the money to help someone. Nita."

"Ah. I understand. Say no more."

"So you won't tell anyone?"

"I won't tell a soul," Madison said. "I can't say I approve, but you have my word that I'll keep your secret."

"Thank you. I mean it."

"So." Madison crossed her arms. "Who is the poor woman you roped into your scheme? Her name is Ruby?"

"Yes. She's an escort. We met at the hotel bar on Saturday night. And trust me, I'm not exploiting her. She's getting several million out of it. It's purely a business arrangement."

Madison smirked. "I'm sure it is."

"I'm serious. We're not even having sex."

"And why not?"

"I don't want things to get complicated."

Besides, Yvonne had certain needs when it came to the women she took into her bed. What she required, what she demanded, of her lovers went far beyond just sex. She needed a woman who was willing to surrender herself to Yvonne completely. Ruby wasn't that woman. Although it was clear that she was far from innocent, it was unlikely she could handle Yvonne's twisted tastes. They weren't for the faint of heart.

Madison didn't look convinced, but she didn't press any further. "Does this mean you need a plus one for the wedding?"

Yvonne hadn't even thought about that yet. Madison's wedding was still a couple of months away. "It will look odd if I don't take Ruby with me. I'll speak to her about it."

"Let me know. It shouldn't be any trouble to squeeze her in. I'll talk to Blair about it." Madison smiled. "She'll be excited to hear you've coupled up. We'll have to have you and Ruby over for dinner sometime."

Yvonne rolled her eyes and changed the subject to something work-related. However, the others would be here soon, and she'd need to tell them about Ruby. Fortunately, she wasn't quite as close to them as Madison, so they'd be far easier to lie to.

What was Ruby up to right now? Yvonne had told her to make herself at home, but she couldn't imagine Ruby doing that. In the short time they'd known each other, Yvonne had gotten the impression that Ruby would simply do whatever she thought would please Yvonne.

It was starting to get to Yvonne. She liked nothing more than a woman who wanted to please her. But with Ruby, it was just an act. Yvonne knew that.

But that didn't make it any less enticing.

She shook her head. Yvonne wasn't going to go down that road with Ruby, and she certainly wasn't interested in anything romantic with the woman. Yvonne wasn't interested in relationships at all. She didn't need anyone else. She'd gone through her entire life alone.

And that was how she liked it.

CHAPTER 5

"Let's get down to business." Yvonne gestured toward the couch at the other side of the coffee table. "Have a seat."

Ruby sat down. It was telling that the first thing Yvonne had done after arriving home from work was 'summon' Ruby to the living room for a formal discussion. Was Yvonne going to behave so coolly toward Ruby for the entire year? That was going to get on Ruby's nerves quickly.

Yvonne reached for the bottle of scotch on a nearby side table, offering Ruby a glass. Ruby declined. Yvonne poured herself a glass before settling back in her seat.

She pushed a sheet of paper across the coffee table toward Ruby. "I drew up a contract outlining our agreement. I'll give you some time to look over it, then we'll sign it later tonight."

"Sounds good to me." Ruby skimmed the contract. There was nothing surprising in it.

Yvonne crossed her legs. "Now, about our cover story."

"Right. I haven't had a chance to think about it yet." Ruby

had spent the day settling in and shopping for essentials. She'd only gotten home half an hour ago and had barely had time to order takeout before Yvonne had arrived.

"I've come up with some ideas myself. The simplest way to make sure we don't slip up is to tell the truth as much as possible. If there are any elements of our history that we can use, we'll stick to those."

Ruby nodded. "That's a good idea."

"I already told my friends about you," Yvonne said. "We work together, so it was unavoidable. I wasn't specific about the details. I told them we met in Vegas a couple of years ago, which is plausible enough."

"Do you go to Vegas a lot? You don't seem the type."

"I travel for work regularly. I go to Vegas often enough. It's a good place to do business. All the money and decadence help prospective investors loosen up." Yvonne took a swig of her drink. "There's a certain type of person who is in their element when surrounded by luxury and excess. Why not take advantage of it?"

Ruby twisted a lock of hair around her finger absently. "Are you one of those types?"

"I'm not so easily impressed," Yvonne said. "Now, where were we?"

Clearly, Ruby's attempts to lighten the mood were falling flat. She was just trying to get Yvonne to relax a bit. They were stuck together for a year. Ruby had to get Yvonne to open up a bit.

"So, we met in Vegas," Yvonne continued. "And since then, we've been casually seeing each other. You became something of a lover. I got into the habit of flying you out to meet me for company whenever I traveled."

"That's believable too? That you'd fly a lover to wherever you were, just to see them?"

"It's believable to anyone who knows me. When it comes to women, I'm quite picky. If I find someone I'm compatible with, I like to keep her on hand. If that means flying her across the country when I need her, I won't hesitate to do that."

"Someone you're compatible with?"

"Let's just say, my tastes are very… specific."

It was obvious that Yvonne wasn't referring to her tastes in appearance or personality. In Ruby's line of work, she'd seen it all, from the tamest to the most scandalous kinks.

Ruby sucked her lip. What was it that Yvonne was into?

"Back to the matter at hand," Yvonne said. "After a year or so of casually seeing each other, we both began to feel like what was between us was more than just physical." She paused. "However, we were afraid to confess our true feelings."

Yvonne spoke as if she were discussing a business deal. Ruby wondered if Yvonne had spoken to her friends about their marriage the same way. She didn't sound convincing at all.

"So, when we met up in Vegas over the weekend, we got blind drunk, drunk enough to finally talk about how we felt, and ended up having a quickie marriage. After we sobered up, we discussed the situation and we decided we wanted to stay married, so I brought you here to live with me. Again, there's that element of truth." Yvonne folded her hands in her lap. "So that's what I've told my friends. We'll need to build upon the story, add some details. But that's the foundation of our back story."

"That works for me," Ruby said. "So, we should probably tell each other about ourselves. Our backgrounds and so on. We should know the details of each other's lives, being married and all." And if Ruby was lucky, talking about themselves would get Yvonne to loosen up a little.

"Good idea," Yvonne said. "Why don't you start?"

"Okay. I'm twenty-five, although I usually don't admit that to my clients. I grew up in a town a few hours from Vegas, moved to Vegas when I turned eighteen, and I've been there ever since. Not sure what else there is to say. I should mention, my real name's Ruth."

"I know. It's on the marriage certificate. Is Ruby just a name you use for work?"

"Kind of," Ruby said. "I started using it because the name Ruth isn't very glamorous, and it stuck. Nobody calls me Ruth anymore."

"Ruby it is," Yvonne said. "Do you have any family?"

"Mom, Dad, and four older brothers. Things were rowdy growing up. What about you?"

"My father died ten years ago. My mother passed when I was young."

"Oh, I'm sorry."

"It was a long time ago." Yvonne's voice remained flat. "I have other family. A half-brother and a stepmother." The way she stressed 'half' and 'step' suggested she wasn't exactly close to them. "As for everything else, I'm thirty-four, and I grew up here in the city. I went to college here too."

Ruby nodded. "Well, I already know what you do for work, but what about me? If people ask about my job, what should we tell them?"

"What do you want to tell them? I have no issues with being married to an escort. You don't have to hide it if you don't want to."

Ruby frowned. So Yvonne had no qualms about Ruby's occupation. And Ruby had already surmised that Yvonne wasn't the type to let emotions or vague, old-fashioned notions of morality get in the way of something as simple and physical as sex.

So why was she so insistent that she didn't want anything physical with Ruby?

Ruby returned to the conversation at hand. "We should come up with something else. Not everyone is as open-minded as you are about my job. Plus, my being an escort will just make people less likely to believe our marriage is real."

"You're right," Yvonne said. "Do you have any suggestions?"

"I sometimes tell people I'm a waitress. I actually was a waitress for a while recently. I took a break from the escort thing after, well…" Ruby pushed down the unease suddenly bubbling up inside her. "It's not important. Anyway, it wouldn't be a stretch to say I was a waitress." She gave Yvonne a cheeky smile. "Obviously, I retired once I found myself a wealthy wife."

"All right. You're a waitress." Yvonne paused. "How did you end up in your line of work? Escorting, that is."

Ruby shrugged. "I moved to Vegas after high school to take a job as a waitress. I was working at one of the restaurants on the strip and I became friends with a regular who was an escort. We'd talk about her job, and it sounded like something I could do, so I gave it a try, and here I am."

"That's it?"

"Do I need a better reason?" Ruby raised an eyebrow. "Or is it because you think only someone desperate or troubled could end up as an escort?"

Yvonne tensed. "That's not what I'm saying. I didn't mean to offend you. It's an unusual profession, that's all."

"I'm just messing with you. But for the record, I don't come from a 'troubled' background. My childhood was great. And my waitressing job, it was well paying with all the tips, but escorting paid even better, and it's far less demanding. There's no desperation involved. And it's a fun job. I get to meet all kinds of interesting people."

"Your clients," Yvonne said. "Are most of them men?"

Ruby nodded. "Women who are interested in hiring female escorts are few and far between. Half of them are just bored rich ladies wanting a taste of the sapphic side. But the female clients who are actually into women have always been my favorites. They appreciate me more."

"So you're actually interested in women? It's not just the job?"

"Women, men, anyone really. Even though this is a job, the attraction is always genuine. I choose my own clients, and I only choose clients I'm attracted to on some level."

Yvonne studied her. "Does that include me?"

Ruby's skin prickled, Yvonne's voice enthralling her. "Like I said, I only choose clients I'm attracted to."

Silence sizzled in the air between them. Yvonne's gaze didn't leave Ruby's. What was going on behind those hypnotic eyes? Everything about Yvonne was impenetrable, from her expression to her words, to the way she held herself. Ruby usually found it easy to read people, but Yvonne was a complete mystery.

Ruby broke the silence. "There's something I want to ask you."

"Go ahead," Yvonne said.

Ruby's heart began to race. "Is there anything else you want from me?"

Yvonne's lips opened ever so slightly. Their eyes still locked, Ruby caught a glimpse of something in Yvonne's, the faintest ember of desire, just like when they'd shared that first glance in the bar in Vegas.

But it only lasted a moment.

"I've already told you what I want," Yvonne said. "I want you to be my wife to the outside world."

"Only to the outside world?" Ruby asked.

"Yes."

"I'm only asking because most people who hire escorts are looking for something more than that."

"I'm not interested in that kind of arrangement."

"Right," Ruby said. "But I've noticed you haven't actually said you're not interested in *me*."

Yvonne stiffened. "That's not relevant. This is a purely business agreement."

Ruby held back a smile. "Right, because you don't 'do' escorts? Is that because of those 'specific tastes' of yours? Nothing fazes me. Trust me, I've seen it all."

Yvonne scoffed. "No, you haven't."

"Yes, I have." Ruby rested her chin on her hands, examining Yvonne. "So what is it that you're into? Do you have a foot fetish? Do you like to make women dress in schoolgirl outfits? Do you like to tie women up?"

Yvonne spoke in a firm voice. "It doesn't matter what I like. I told you. I'm not interested. I don't pay for sex. And even if I did, that's the last thing I'd want from *you!*"

Ruby flinched, a stinging feeling growing in her chest. Clearly, she'd pushed Yvonne too far. "Okay. Message received."

Yvonne let out an exasperated sigh. "Ruby-"

Ruby held up her hands. "I hear you loud and clear. Forget I said anything."

"Ruby."

The doorbell rang.

"That's the takeout I ordered." Without giving Yvonne a chance to respond, Ruby got up and left the room.

She headed to the door, a sinking feeling in her stomach. Was she actually upset that Yvonne wanted to keep things business? It wouldn't be the first time a client had wanted an arrangement that was entirely platonic. Besides, it was a *good* thing. It made Ruby's job simpler, decreasing the risk of her getting emotionally involved. So why did Yvonne's words bother her so much?

There was only one explanation. Ruby wanted Yvonne. Badly.

And considering their complicated circumstances, and the dangerous way that Yvonne seemed to be able to get under Ruby's skin, that was *not* a good thing.

CHAPTER 6

It was early afternoon when Ruby returned to Yvonne's apartment. She'd treated herself to lunch at the fanciest restaurant she could find using the credit card Yvonne had given her, simply so she'd have something to do. Now, boredom was setting in again.

She sat down in the living room. It had been a week since she'd signed the contract laying out her agreement with Yvonne. Since then, Ruby had taken advantage of her new status as Yvonne Maxwell's 'wife'. She'd embraced a life of luxury, ordering expensive food and furnishing herself with a whole new wardrobe. But it had only taken a few days before the novelty had worn off.

Now, Ruby was faced with the reality that she had absolutely nothing to do.

It didn't help that she didn't know a single person in the city other than Yvonne, and Yvonne seemed determined to maintain a professional distance from Ruby. Sure, Yvonne had reiterated that their arrangement was purely business, but with the way Yvonne was behaving, it was like she was going out of her way to avoid Ruby. Yvonne would leave for work early in the morning and would come home late at night, with nothing but a 'good morning' or 'good night' if Ruby happened to be around. Ruby wasn't sure whether to take it personally. Yvonne was a busy woman, and it had been clear from the moment they'd met that Yvonne wasn't a warm, bubbly person.

But this felt like something more.

Ruby recalled the conversation they'd had that first night. *It's the last thing I want from you.* Yvonne's words had been clear. Her behavior, however, was far more ambiguous.

Ruby knew a thing or two about attraction, and Yvonne showed all the signs of wanting Ruby, in her cool, reserved way. When Ruby would walk by late at night in nothing but the oversized t-shirt she slept in, Yvonne's eyes would follow her, before snapping away. When they passed by each other in the hall, Ruby would feel Yvonne's gaze on her. When Ruby would go into the kitchen for breakfast, freshly showered, combing her fingers through her damp hair while she waited for her toast to pop, Yvonne would give her a wide berth but would watch her out the side of her eye.

Ruby sighed. Yvonne was so confusing. Clearly, she wasn't going to warm up to Ruby any time soon. Ruby couldn't rely on Yvonne to keep her occupied.

However, Ruby didn't know what to do with herself. She had no hobbies, no interests, no way to pass the time. It was like she was just this blank slate of a person. She had no friends to call, no one to talk to. Not anymore.

Things hadn't always been this way. It had been a slow, gradual thing. And it had all started with *him*.

Over time, as they'd become more than just client and escort, she'd changed. She'd become who he wanted her to be. She hadn't noticed it at the time, that she was losing her identity, her sense of self. And over time, she'd lost touch with everyone else in her life, even her own family. It was all part of his manipulations.

That was all in the past. Ruby was free now. And yet, she didn't know how to deal with her freedom. She felt overwhelmed, completely lost and directionless. She'd felt this way for so long now, ever since she'd left him. That self-assured siren Ruby pretended to be wasn't real. It was a mask to hide all her uncertainties.

She stretched out on the couch. She needed a distraction. As she glanced around the apartment, an idea popped into her mind. Perhaps she could try to find out a little more about Yvonne.

The day Ruby had arrived, she'd checked out every room in the huge apartment, except for Yvonne's bedroom and study. Yvonne kept those doors closed at all times. Perhaps Ruby could find some more hints about the woman inside her spaces. Besides, this apartment was Ruby's home for the next year. It was odd that she lived here, yet she didn't know what some of the rooms looked like. Taking a peek inside them wouldn't hurt.

She got up from the couch and crept to Yvonne's study. Yvonne spent a lot of time inside it. There had to be some clue, some hint inside about what was behind Yvonne's mask.

Ruby turned the door handle. It was unlocked. She

slipped inside and looked around. To her dismay, it was just a regular, boring home office, with a desk in the middle and some bookcases and cabinets. Ruby tiptoed to Yvonne's desk. It had a few folders and documents on it, including the contract she and Ruby had signed. Their marriage certificate was there too, as well as some other papers that looked to be work-related.

Ruby's eyes landed on a check sitting on top of a pile of documents. She picked it up. The check was made out to a 'Nita Chen,' and it was for almost a hundred thousand dollars. That was a lot of money, although it probably wasn't much to Yvonne. Who was Nita and why was Yvonne paying her so much?

She put the check down. It was none of her business who Yvonne gave her money to. Ruby left the room and headed to Yvonne's bedroom at the end of the hall. She opened the door. The bedroom was even more disappointing than the study. It was decorated much like the rest of the house, and just as neat and tidy. So was her bathroom, although it was twice the size of Ruby's. But there were no clues to who Yvonne was in the room.

Ruby shut the door. As she did, she realized that there was another room next to Yvonne's bedroom that she hadn't noticed earlier. How had she missed it?

She opened the door to the room to find another spare bedroom. But unlike the others, which looked rarely used, this bedroom was well decorated and furnished, the bed fully made with linens and extra pillows.

Ruby frowned. Was it a guest room? It was too nice. Too made up. It looked too well used. And the decor in it was different. Whereas the beds in Ruby's room and the master bedroom were made with crisp cotton sheets in neutral, light colors that matched the rest of the house, this bed was made up with dark satin sheets and velvet pillows. The lighting was different too. Darker, softer.

More sensual.

Ruby took a step into the room, then another, not knowing what she was looking for. She simply had this feeling. She walked over to the four-poster bed, running her hands along the satin sheets. Next to the bed were matching nightstands. She opened one of them up.

Her mouth dropped open. Inside the drawer, laid out neatly on a bed of velvet, was an assortment of handcuffs.

Ruby slammed the drawer shut and opened the one below it. More cuffs, this time made of leather. She opened the bottom drawer. Ropes, all neatly coiled, lined up by length and color.

Ruby's heart thudded hard inside her chest. She looked around the room. There was a dresser and a closet on the far wall. She walked over to the dresser and opened the drawers one by one. Two held an assortment of whips. Another was filled with blindfolds, gags, and all kinds of leather straps. Another held an array of intimidating-looking metal tools and restraints. She found more of the same in the closet.

Heat suffused Ruby's entire body. So this was what Yvonne meant about her 'tastes.' Ruby had suspected that Yvonne was the dominant type, but she'd had no idea just how seriously Yvonne took it all.

This had to be why Yvonne kept rebuffing Ruby. Did she think that Ruby wouldn't be interested in all this?

Yvonne couldn't be more wrong.

Ruby picked up a coil of rope from the shelf, letting her fingertips run over the rough fibers. Desire ignited within her. Despite what she'd been through with her last client, everything in this room excited her. She shouldn't have wanted this. But she did.

Ruby wanted a taste of what Yvonne had to offer. And while she wasn't sure if Yvonne was willing to give her one, one thing was certain.

Ruby was going to make sure Yvonne knew how much she wanted this.

~

Ruby sat on the bed in the bedroom next to Yvonne's, waiting for her. It was late at night. Yvonne was due home any moment now.

Something fluttered in Ruby's chest. Was she really doing this? Was she making a huge mistake? Would Ruby's actions simply infuriate Yvonne? That was a possibility. Ruby knew she was overstepping. She knew she was pushing Yvonne's boundaries.

But she had to get through to Yvonne.

Faintly, Ruby heard the front door open at the other end of the apartment. Yvonne was home. It was too late to back out now. As Ruby repositioned herself on the bed, Yvonne's footsteps grew louder, before slowing down in the hall. Ruby's pulse raced even faster. Could Yvonne see the light coming from the room? Was she wondering why the door was open?

Did she have any idea of what she was going to find inside?

Ruby held her breath. A second later, Yvonne appeared in the doorway.

Ruby gazed at her from the bed. "I've been waiting for you to come home."

Yvonne froze in place, taking in the scene before her. Scattered on the bed around Ruby was a selection of Yvonne's toys and tools from the drawers and closet. Handcuffs. A blindfold. A coil of rope. A whip. And Ruby had placed herself in the middle as a centerpiece, kneeling with her hands in her lap, looking up at Yvonne from under her eyelashes.

Yvonne's eyes met Ruby's. They burned hot. Was it anger, or something else?

"What are you doing in here?" Yvonne's voice was edged with ice.

"What does it look like?" Ruby gestured around herself. "I found all your toys. And I'm intrigued."

"No." Yvonne shook her head. "No. You need to get out of here."

"Why? And don't say you don't want me."

"I don't want *this*."

Ruby gave her a playful smile. "So you *do* want me?"

Yvonne tore her eyes away from Ruby. "I already told you our arrangement is purely financial. It can't be anything more."

"And why is that?" Ruby crossed her arms, abandoning her attempted display of submissiveness. "I know you're not shy about sex. Everything I've found in this room is proof of that. And I understand what you meant now, about your tastes."

"No, you don't," Yvonne said firmly. "This isn't a game, Ruby!"

"I know that. And I get it. I get what it is that you want. I want that too. Whatever you want from me, I'll give it to you."

"That isn't how this works."

"Then how does it work? Show me. Please."

Yvonne folded her arms over her chest. "No."

Ruby let out a frustrated groan. "I don't understand you! You look at me like you want me, and I want you too, Yvonne. I want this."

Yvonne shook her head. "You have no idea what you're asking of me, Ruby."

"What, do you think I haven't been with anyone who's into kinky stuff before?"

"Not like this. Look at you." Yvonne waved a hand in Ruby's direction. "You don't understand any of this, otherwise you wouldn't be doing what you are now, offering yourself up to me on a platter. You have no idea what you're doing. You're obviously a complete novice."

"Maybe you're right. But you can teach me."

Yvonne shook her head again. "I'm not the right person to teach you. This just demonstrates that. You're rash, controlled by your desires. You need someone who will slowly and carefully ease you into this world. I am *not* that person. I can't be that person for you."

"Why not? What are you afraid of? That you'll hurt me?"

"Physically? No. But there are so many other ways to hurt someone."

"You won't hurt me," Ruby said. "I trust you."

Yvonne scoffed. "You don't even know me."

"You're right. I don't know you, not really." Ruby looked down at the toys on the bed around her. "But I understand what it is you want, on some level. You want control. You want power. You want someone who will give both to you."

Yvonne didn't move or speak, but her eyes, which had shifted from green to brown in the low light, seemed to sizzle.

"And I can tell that you're the kind of person who takes this seriously. I can tell that if I give you control, if I place myself in your hands, you won't abuse that power. I know that you'll take care of me." Ruby fixed her gaze on Yvonne, her voice growing softer. "Yvonne, I want this so badly. I want *you* so badly."

Silence fell between them. Yvonne stared back at Ruby, saying nothing, but Ruby could see the battle going on within her. Yvonne held her body stiff and still, as poised to pounce on Ruby like she was Yvonne's prey.

But when Yvonne finally spoke, it was with an icy calm that sent a shiver through Ruby's core.

"Show me."

Ruby blinked. "Show you?"

"Show me how much you want this."

"I will. Anything."

Silence fell between them. Ruby awaited Yvonne's instructions, the sound of her pounding heart filling her head.

Still standing in place in the doorway, half in shadow, Yvonne lifted her chin and looked into Ruby's eyes, before speaking a single word.

"Crawl."

A prickly heat rose to Ruby's skin. She stared back at

Yvonne, the cold fire in the woman's eyes enthralling. She didn't try to fight it. She was powerless to do anything but follow Yvonne's command.

Ruby slipped off the bed and dropped to her knees.

Her palms hit the wooden floorboards.

She cast her eyes down, and she began to crawl toward Yvonne.

Deep within her, desire flared to life. As she crawled to the other woman, the space separating them seemed to grow even more vast. But slowly, on her hands and knees, Ruby crossed the distance between them.

She reached Yvonne's heeled feet, but she didn't look up. She simply knelt there, her head bowed and her eyes downcast, her heart thundering in her chest. Seconds stretched out. Yvonne was still and silent. Ruby remained on the floor, prostrating herself before the other woman, awaiting her command.

But instead, Yvonne took a step back, then another.

Then she turned on her heel and strode out the door, shutting it behind her.

CHAPTER 7

Yvonne looked at the time. Almost 8 p.m. It was a Friday, so the office was nearly empty, save for a few stragglers. Yvonne would normally be heading home around this time too, but she had no intention of leaving any time soon. Not with Ruby in her apartment.

She turned back to her laptop, trying to focus, but she couldn't stop playing that scene over and over in her mind. Ruby, kneeling on the bed before her, surrounded by Yvonne's toys. Ruby, looking back at her, her eyes filled with a desperate yearning. Ruby, on her hands and knees, at Yvonne's feet…

Yvonne shut her laptop. She needed a distraction.

She left her office, heading toward the office of Mistress's CFO. If Yvonne was lucky, Lydia would still be around. Unlike the rest of the members of the executive team who had started Mistress together, Lydia had only joined them recently, although she'd worked with Mistress as a consultant for longer. Yvonne didn't know her very well, but she had a question about finance, Lydia's area of expertise.

Yvonne reached Lydia's office. The auburn-haired woman was still inside, packing up her desk. Yvonne knocked on the door. Lydia waved her in.

"Do you have a moment?" Yvonne asked. "I'll make it quick. I have a finance question, but it's personal, not business."

Lydia shut her bag. "Go ahead."

"I need to set aside a sum of money for someone without her spouse being able to touch it. How would I go about doing that?"

Lydia frowned. "That's a little complex. Normally, I'd suggest you create a trust, but in case of a married couple, both spouses would be legally entitled to the money in it. I'd recommend you speak to legal, especially given the circumstances of your marriage."

"My marriage?" Did Lydia think Yvonne was talking about herself? "This isn't about me. This is for someone else. A friend."

"If you say so."

"I mean it. I want to give someone money she can use for her family's needs, but I don't want her *husband* to have access to it."

"I see." Lydia paused in thought. "She has children?"

"Yes."

"In that case, a trust for the children could work, with their mother as the sole trustee. If you include a provision that the money can only be used for expenses related to the children and their care, it will prevent her husband from getting his hands on it. The definition of 'care' is broad enough that there's a lot of wiggle room, so she'll still be able to spend the money relatively freely. But once again, I'm not a lawyer. You definitely need to speak with one."

"I will," Yvonne said. "I'm just looking into options right now. Thank you for your help."

"Any time." Lydia paused. "Is everything all right?"

Yvonne nodded. "Just trying to help a friend."

Fortunately, Lydia didn't pry. Yvonne appreciated that about her. She was cordial but reserved.

Yvonne nodded to her. "I'll see you on Monday."

She left Lydia's office and headed back to her own, taking a seat behind her desk and opening her laptop again. Yvonne didn't actually have any work to do because ever since Ruby had moved in, she'd been staying late at the office. She'd gotten all her extra work done already.

But after the other night, the idea of simply being around Ruby was torturous. What had passed between them that night—Ruby, offering herself up to Yvonne, Ruby, on her hands and knees at Yvonne's command?

It had only made Yvonne want her even more.

Yvonne let out a long, hard breath. Her command had been a challenge, one she'd given to Ruby with the expectation that Ruby would back down.

But Ruby hadn't backed down. She'd done exactly what Yvonne had commanded, without hesitation. And she'd remained at Yvonne's feet, unspeaking, unmoving, the perfect, willing, eager submissive.

Yvonne closed her eyes, picturing it again. There had been something different about Ruby that night. Something about her in that moment that had stood out to Yvonne.

However, Yvonne couldn't quite put her finger on what exactly it was.

It didn't matter. She had to stop thinking about Ruby. The more Yvonne thought about her, the more she was tempted by her. But getting involved with Ruby in any way, let alone such an intimate way, would be a mistake. For starters, Yvonne was paying Ruby, which introduced all kinds of complications. They were stuck together for a year. If things got awkward between them, it would be an uncomfortable year. And if something went wrong, Yvonne's inheritance would be at risk.

But the most important reason was exactly what Yvonne had said to Ruby that night. Yvonne wasn't the right person to introduce Ruby to the twisted world of BDSM, especially not Yvonne's brand of it. Yvonne was in too deep, her tastes too extreme. Ruby was a novice, and Yvonne didn't have the patience to hold her hand through it. She wasn't that kind of Domme.

The door to Yvonne's office opened. She looked up to find Madison strolling into the room, her coat and bag on her arm.

"You're still here?" Madison asked.

"I have work to do," Yvonne lied.

Madison sat down in the chair in front of Yvonne's desk. "You've stayed late every day this week."

"I've been busy. The shareholder meeting is coming up. I need to present them with our strategy for the next quarter."

"Doesn't your wife miss you?"

Yvonne pressed her lips together. "She's *not* my wife."

"*I* know that. But the rest of the world doesn't." Madison

crossed her arms. "The two of you are newlyweds. It's awfully suspicious that you're working all the time instead of spending time with her. Wasn't the whole point of this charade for everyone else to think the two of you are a real couple? You should be rushing home every day to be with her, not hanging back at work for hours."

The same thought had occurred to Yvonne, but she'd ignored it.

"So tell me. What's going on? Why are you avoiding going home?"

Yvonne closed her laptop and pushed it aside. "Let's just say, Ruby has been getting under my skin."

"I can't say I'm surprised."

Yvonne frowned. "What's that supposed to mean?"

"You're not exactly a people person," Madison said. "And all of a sudden, you're sharing your life and space with a stranger. It's no surprise that tensions are flaring."

That was true. There was plenty of tension between Yvonne and Ruby.

"Yvonne, if you're going to be stuck with Ruby for a year, you need to figure out a way to coexist. No, you need to do more than just coexist. You need to get along. Hiding in the office isn't going to help with that."

Yvonne scoffed. "Are you seriously lecturing me on how to fix my 'marriage?' I thought you didn't approve of it in the first place."

"I don't. But I know you well enough. I know that you're too stubborn to do anything other than see this ridiculous charade through to the end. So you need to make it as easy as possible, which means you need to make nice with Ruby." Before Yvonne could protest, Madison stood. "I need to get going. Blair left an hour ago, and unlike you, I'm not about to leave her waiting up for me all night. Just think about what I said. Make nice with Ruby. And *go home*."

Yvonne muttered a goodbye. Madison left her office.

Yvonne opened her laptop up again. 'Making nice' with Ruby was *not* an option, no matter how much Yvonne wanted to.

That image flashed in her mind again. Ruby on the bed, in nothing but a simple black dress, her hair falling down her shoulders like gold silk. All Yvonne's toys scattered on the bed around her, a tempting cornucopia of tools with which Yvonne could lavish endless agonizing pleasures upon her. Yvonne should have been furious that Ruby had invaded her space, gone through her things, touched the precious toys she so painstakingly cared for and stored. Yet Yvonne had been too deeply distracted by her desire for Ruby to care.

As Yvonne played the scene over again in her mind, she finally realized what that change, that shift in Ruby had been that night. It was as if the mask Ruby wore, the one that transformed her into a seductive fantasy, had fallen away. At that moment, Yvonne had gotten a glimpse of the real Ruby.

It had been the real Ruby who had said *I want this*. It had been the real Ruby who had pleaded for Yvonne to teach her. It had been the real Ruby who had gotten on her hands and knees and crawled to Yvonne's feet.

And that side of Ruby was even more irresistible than the woman Yvonne had met at the bar.

Ruby stared at herself in the mirror as she brushed her teeth. It was late, almost midnight, and she was alone in the apartment. There was no sign of Yvonne at all.

As far as Ruby was concerned, that was a good thing. Since that night in Yvonne's 'playroom,' Ruby had been avoiding Yvonne. However, she suspected she didn't need to avoid Yvonne at all. Yvonne had been spending even more time out of the apartment than before. Ruby had no doubt that she was the reason.

Crawl. Despite all the days that had passed, Yvonne's command still haunted Ruby. She kept replaying the scene in her head, over and over and over. She'd been so helpless under Yvonne's gaze, unable to resist the urge to do exactly what Yvonne had told her. And the worst part?

Ruby had enjoyed every second of it.

Ruby rinsed out her mouth and splashed some cold water on her burning face. Just thinking about that moment gave her the same thrill that she'd felt that night. Ruby had always had submissive tendencies. She liked giving up control, liked letting others take charge in the bedroom. But it was one thing to have someone spank her during sex, or to mess around with a pair of handcuffs. This was something else entirely. That moment when Ruby had gotten on her knees and crawled to Yvonne's feet—it had triggered something inside her, that dark, insatiable side of her that craved submission. And she may have been imagining it, but she had sensed a shift in Yvonne too. What had passed between them?

It had felt so right.

But Yvonne had turned her back on Ruby. She'd left Ruby kneeling on the floor. And that stung.

Ruby headed back into her bedroom. It was time for yet another night spent lying awake, wondering if she'd made a mistake by agreeing to this sham of a marriage. The situation had been bad enough before, but Ruby had made things even worse. She should never have tried to seduce Yvonne.

Could she really survive a year of this? Of living with a woman who was equal parts sexy and cold? Who awakened all of Ruby's fantasies, who pushed all her buttons?

Shedding everything but a t-shirt and her underwear, Ruby slipped into her bed then turned off the light. She shut her eyes, desperately willing sleep to come and save her from everything she was feeling. Regret. Hurt.

Desire.

Ruby sighed. Despite it all, despite Yvonne literally turning her back on Ruby, she wanted Yvonne even more.

As the beginnings of sleep finally began to take her, Ruby heard the faint sound of the front door opening at the other end of the apartment. So Yvonne was home. Ruby didn't care. As Yvonne's footsteps echoed down the hall, growing closer, Ruby rolled over and pulled the covers up over her, waiting for Yvonne to pass and continue to her bedroom.

But instead, the footsteps stopped at Ruby's door.

Ruby's heart thumped. She waited. Five seconds, then ten, then twenty. But all she heard was silence. Perhaps Yvonne had already moved on and Ruby hadn't heard her? Ruby turned over in bed again, but she just couldn't shake the feeling nagging at her.

Quietly, Ruby switched on the lamp, got out of bed, and padded to the door. She turned the door handle and opened it wide.

Yvonne. Yvonne was standing in the doorway.

Ruby looked at the woman's face. In the dim light, it was shrouded in darkness, but Ruby could see that it was set like stone, even more expressionless than usual.

But within Yvonne's eyes, a fire smoldered that set every part of Ruby's body alight.

"Yvonne," Ruby whispered. "I-"

"Don't speak."

Ruby fell silent. Yvonne gazed back at her, probing, piercing, stripping away all of Ruby's layers, until all that was left was the part of her that had answered Yvonne's command to crawl that night. Ruby cast her eyes down, unable to bear the heat of Yvonne's gaze.

Yvonne took Ruby's chin in her fingers and tipped Ruby's face up to hers. Before Ruby could take a breath, Yvonne's lips were on hers in a deep, demanding kiss.

Ruby crumbled.

CHAPTER 8

Ruby closed her eyes, her lips and body crushing back against Yvonne's. She clung to Yvonne's dress, holding onto her while pulling her closer, overcome by the woman's relentless kiss. If she'd had any doubt that Yvonne wanted her, it was gone now.

Their lips still locked, Yvonne pushed her way into the room, backing Ruby against the bed. Ruby fell upon it, taking Yvonne down with her.

Yvonne straightened up, staring down at Ruby, her eyes blazing with hunger. "The other night," she said, her voice firm and low. "In my playroom. Everything you did, everything you said. It wasn't an act."

"No," Ruby replied. "It wasn't."

She sat up, reaching for Yvonne, wanting to pull her in and kiss her again. But Yvonne pushed Ruby's shoulders back down to the bed, holding her there with the light pressure of her hand.

"What you did that night. Trying to seduce me. Trying to get me to give you what you want. It was unacceptable." She dragged her hand down Ruby's cheek and the side of her neck. "You need to understand what I expect from my submissive."

Her submissive. The idea made Ruby just as hot as Yvonne's kiss.

"You were right about one thing," Yvonne said. "About what I want. Power. Control, complete and unfettered."

She drew her hand down the center of Ruby's chest, all the way to her lower stomach. A flood of desire went through her. Yvonne snaked her hand up underneath Ruby's shirt, sliding it up to Ruby's bare chest.

"But I don't just want someone who will hand me control. What I need is someone who will surrender to me completely."

"I understand," Ruby whispered.

"I don't think you do. You want someone who will fulfill your desires, all those wicked little fantasies in your head." Yvonne skimmed her fingers over Ruby's breasts. "You want someone who will serve *your* needs."

Ruby let out a shuddering breath. Her nipples were already hard peaks.

"Is that what you want?" Yvonne dipped down, her lips caressing Ruby's ear. "Or do you want a Mistress to serve?"

Ruby trembled. "I want to serve you."

"Then you need to understand what it is you'll be giving me. You will be mine to command. Your mind. Your body." Yvonne rolled her fingertips over Ruby's nipple. "Your pleasure."

Ruby let out a sharp breath. Yvonne pinched Ruby's nipple gently, sending a jolt of pleasure through her. Her chest hitched, her hands splaying on the bed beneath at either side of her.

"Is that what you want?" Yvonne asked.

"Yes," Ruby said softly.

Yvonne's other hand crept down Ruby's stomach, lower and lower until she reached the peak of Ruby's thighs. Ruby parted her legs reflexively as Yvonne traced her fingers over Ruby's lower lips through her panties. Ruby exhaled softly.

"Then I'll show you," Yvonne said. "I'll teach you."

"Yes," Ruby murmured.

Yvonne drew her hand back up, slipping it inside Ruby's panties. She pushed her finger into Ruby's slit, stroking gently. "You will exist to serve me. Not the other way around."

Pleasure lanced through Ruby's body. "Yes."

Yvonne circled Ruby's aching clit with her fingertip. Ruby let out a fevered gasp, her thighs trembling.

"Your pleasure will be mine to give." Yvonne withdrew her hand from Ruby's panties. "And to take."

Ruby bit back a whimper. "Yes."

"*You* will be mine."

"Yes…"

Yvonne grabbed the waistband of Ruby's panties and tugged them down Ruby's legs before parting them again. She slid her fingers between Ruby's thighs once more, running them down to Ruby's entrance. She circled it slowly, teasing her.

This time, Ruby couldn't stop the whimper escaping from her lips. She looked back up at Yvonne, the other woman's eyes dark and lustful.

"I will be your everything," Yvonne whispered.

Yes. But Ruby found she couldn't speak. She couldn't think, couldn't breathe, she was so consumed with need. She closed her eyes, her head rolling back, her body yearning for Yvonne.

Finally, Yvonne entered her, piercing her to her core. Ruby arched up, pleasure rippling through her with every stroke of Yvonne's fingers. Was this a dream? Had Ruby fallen asleep and imagined Yvonne coming to her door? No, Ruby wasn't imagining the weight of Yvonne on her, the heat of the woman's skin against hers. She wasn't imagining the way Yvonne felt inside her. She wasn't imagining Yvonne's soft, rhythmic breaths in her ear. She wasn't imagining the way her body screamed for Yvonne's touch.

And Ruby wanted to touch Yvonne too, to feel her, to explore her, to hold her. But Yvonne had been clear. She demanded control.

And Ruby was powerless to do anything but give it to her.

"Yes," she murmured. "Oh, yes…"

As Yvonne delved inside her, Ruby let herself get swept away in the tempest that was the other woman. Everything about Yvonne was overwhelming. Her firm, velvet voice. Her tender but insistent touch. Her undeniably dominant presence.

Yvonne thrust harder, the whole room shaking. Ruby gripped the sheets beneath her, holding on against Yvonne's disorienting passion until at last, she couldn't take anymore.

"Yvonne," she cried. "Oh-"

A spark went off deep within, crackling through her like electricity. She rose up into Yvonne, her body seeking the other woman's. Yvonne's lips collided with Ruby's as she continued to work away inside her, drawing out every last bit of pleasure from Ruby's body, until finally, she went limp.

Yvonne eased away, letting her lips linger on Ruby's, her kiss transforming from furious to soft. Ruby dissolved into her, a part of her hoping that Yvonne would draw her into an embrace.

But instead, Yvonne broke away and looked down at her, an unreadable expression on her face. Tentatively, Ruby reached up and placed a hand on Yvonne's cheek, searching Yvonne's eyes. Ruby's heart pounded loudly in the still, silent room. Was Yvonne trying to figure out what was going on in Ruby's head too?

After a moment, Yvonne brought her hand up to Ruby's, pulling it from her cheek and letting it fall to the bed. Her voice cut into the silence.

"Good night, Ruby. I'll see you tomorrow."

Ruby blinked, still in a daze. "Good night?"

Yvonne got up from the bed and walked silently to the door. "One more thing. If you ever, *ever* try anything like what you did the other night again, I'll do far worse than make you crawl."

Yvonne left the room, shutting the door behind her.

CHAPTER 9

When Ruby awoke the next morning, she was only half certain that the previous night hadn't been a dream. The abrupt way it had ended certainly hadn't helped. Once again, Yvonne had walked out the door on her.

But unlike last time, Ruby was certain she'd gotten through to Yvonne. Now, she was certain Yvonne wanted Ruby's submission just as much as Ruby wanted to give it to her.

Ruby's mind went back to all the things she'd found in Yvonne's playroom. All those tools and toys, the ropes, and whips, and cuffs. She wanted a taste of it all. And she wanted it with Yvonne.

Ruby's stomach stirred. She didn't like that she felt so strongly toward a client, even if it was just physical. It was dangerous. But this was different. Yvonne was different. She wasn't like *him*. Hadn't she already shown that?

Ruby pushed the thought aside and got out of bed. As she left her bedroom, the faint sound of the shower running in Yvonne's bathroom reached her. The life of leisure Ruby had been living meant that she'd lost track of the days. It was the weekend. Yvonne didn't have work.

The two of them would have to face what had happened the night before sooner rather than later.

Ruby headed to the kitchen and made herself a quick breakfast. She was sitting at the counter eating her toast when Yvonne strolled in. She was dressed relatively casually in a simple dark blue dress, her dark hair loose. She looked so radiant. So confident. So captivating.

"Good morning." Yvonne spoke in her usual businesslike manner. "Did you sleep well?"

"Y-yes," Ruby replied.

Yvonne took a mug from the cupboard and poured herself some coffee. "When you have the time, there's something we need to discuss."

Ruby pushed aside the remains of her breakfast, her hunger replaced with nerves. "I have time now."

"Let's go to my study."

Ruby followed Yvonne to her study, like an employee called into her boss's office. No, more like a student called to the principal's office.

"Take a seat," Yvonne said.

Ruby sat. Yvonne shut the door and took a seat at the other side of the desk. On top of the desk between them was a thick document stapled together.

"Here." Yvonne slid it toward Ruby. "It's a contract."

Ruby frowned. "Didn't we already sign the contract?"

"This is a contract of a different kind."

Ruby picked up the papers and scanned the first page.

Agreement between Yvonne Maxwell ("the Dominant") and Ruth "Ruby" Scott ("the submissive").

Ruby flicked through the rest of the pages. What the hell was this? There were over a dozen sections, all with bold headings. *Roles. Responsibilities. Areas of Control. Limits.* There was an entire page dedicated to different bondage-related activities alone. There had to be at least twenty pages in total.

"You want me to sign this?" When had Yvonne even written it? This morning? What kind of woman fucked someone and then drew up a contract the next day?

The woman Ruby was married to, apparently.

"Not immediately," Yvonne said. "I want you to take your time and go through it thoroughly. And it's all negotiable. We can discuss anything you have reservations about or anything you don't understand. I've left space for you to add in your limits. That's any activity that's off the table completely. You'll also need to choose a safeword."

Ruby blinked. "Is all this necessary?" There were so many rules. Did they really have to have it all in writing?

What would happen if Ruby broke one?

"Have you changed your mind about wanting to do this?" Yvonne asked.

"No. Not at all." Yet, Ruby had some reservations. Could she really trust Yvonne, this virtual stranger she'd somehow ended up married to?

"Then yes, this is necessary." Yvonne folded her hands in front of her. "I want you to understand that this contract isn't about obligations. It's about setting clear boundaries and limits, as well as expectations. That applies to both of us."

Ruby glanced down at the contract again. All the language was so businesslike. That was typical of Yvonne.

"You also need to understand that having a contract doesn't mean we don't have to communicate about everything. We'll still need to discuss any issues that arise." Yvonne's expression grew more serious. "Ruby, you're new at all this. For everything between us to work, we need to be completely open with each other. If you're feeling uncomfortable or overwhelmed, tell me. If you change your mind about anything, or you realize you don't want to do something we've previously agreed upon, tell me. Whatever you're thinking and feeling, you need to tell me. What we're doing is intense. Feelings get magnified, people can get hurt. I require complete honesty from you, and I will give you the same."

Ruby had no problem being honest about her feelings and needs. However, she was already keeping something from Yvonne. The lie she'd told was small, more of an omission than anything, but it hid a bigger secret, one that she knew Yvonne would want to know about.

But if Ruby told her the truth, would Yvonne put a stop to the arrangement they were about to enter into?

Yvonne examined her. "What are you thinking?"

"Nothing," Ruby replied.

Yvonne crossed her arms. "Ruby, I just told you I require complete honesty from you. Tell me the truth. How does this all make you feel?"

Ruby thought for a moment. "At first, it made me nervous. A contract? That seems so formal. But the more I think about it, it's reassuring." Yvonne had thought this all through. She was being cautious and careful, and she cared about Ruby's well-being and her safety. "It makes me feel like I can trust you."

Yvonne gave her a small nod. "That's good. That's the point. Now, I want you to go away and read the contract. Make a list of your own limits. Take note of anything you want to negotiate. If you have any questions, ask me. We'll finalize the contract when you're ready. I want you to take your time to understand what you're getting into."

Ruby nodded.

"You may go."

Ruby got up and headed to the door, contract in hand. As she opened the door, Yvonne spoke.

"And Ruby?"

"Yes?"

"Until that contract has been signed, nothing will happen between us."

Oh. Ruby hesitated. "And after I sign it? What happens then?"

Yvonne's lips curled up slightly. "Then the teaching begins."

CHAPTER 10

Yvonne pulled up in front of a large suburban house. Between work and her impromptu marriage, she'd been far too busy to make the long-overdue trip to visit the person dearest to her.

Nita.

As Yvonne parked the car, she caught sight of the wedding ring on her finger. She'd finally gotten used to the feel of it on her hand. Although she and Ruby had been married for a few weeks now, it had only been a week since that night that had bound them together in an entirely different way.

Ruby hadn't yet signed the second contract. She was taking her time. Yvonne had thought Ruby had gotten cold feet until she'd started asking Yvonne questions about the contract and all the kinky little details within it. And every time she did, she would ponder Yvonne's answers while looking at Yvonne with eager, lust-filled eyes.

It was making Yvonne regret having told Ruby that

nothing could happen between them until they finalized the contract. Yvonne had almost cracked, more than once, but she'd stuck to her guns. She had to take control of the situation. What had happened that night in Ruby's bedroom had been entirely unplanned. Yvonne still didn't know what had possessed her to stop at Ruby's door.

The contract was as much for Yvonne as it was for Ruby. She needed to have clear limits and boundaries in all areas of her life. It kept things simple. If she and Ruby were going to be stuck together for a year, the last thing they needed was for things to get any more complicated than they already were.

Yvonne stared at the ring, wondering whether to take it off. She didn't want to have to explain everything to Nita, and there was very little chance of her finding out about Yvonne's marriage through the grapevine. Nita was very much separate from the rest of Yvonne's life. But at the same time, Yvonne couldn't keep something this big from her.

Without removing the ring, Yvonne got out of her car and headed toward the house. Nita's family had lived here for years, but they were at risk of losing it all. Yvonne wasn't going to let that happen.

She rang the doorbell and waited. A minute later, the door opened. A short Chinese woman, her face faintly lined with age, stood in the doorway.

"Yvonne," she said. "What a lovely surprise."

"Nita," Yvonne said. "Sorry I haven't been by for a while."

"It's fine." Nita spoke with the barest hint of an accent. "You're a busy woman. You don't have to worry about me. Why don't you come in?"

Yvonne followed Nita inside. The house was quiet. There was no sign of Nita's husband, Mark, or her kids. At Nita's urging, Yvonne took a seat at the kitchen table. Nita poured them both some tea and sat down across from her.

She gave Yvonne an affectionate smile. "Xiǎo táo. It's good to see you."

Yvonne felt a spark of warmth in her chest. *Xiǎo táo* was Mandarin for *little peach*. It was what Yvonne's mother had called her as a child. Apparently, when Yvonne was a baby, she'd been so chubby that her cheeks had looked like two round, ripe peaches. Yvonne's mother had been Chinese. However, her father's side of the family had Scottish roots, which her father had taken very seriously, proudly displaying their family crest over the mantelpiece in their home. Aside from her dark hair, Yvonne took after her father, so most people didn't realize she was Chinese at all. That part of her, the part which came from her mother, was virtually invisible. She occasionally got comments about her vaguely 'exotic' looks, but she'd learned long ago to shut down any such comments with an icy glare.

Nita began fussing over Yvonne like usual. "Are you hungry? I'll make you something."

"I'm fine," Yvonne said. "I'm not ten anymore. You don't need to feed me every time I so much as drop by."

"Yes, I do. If I know you, you haven't been looking after yourself. When was the last time you sat down and had a home-cooked meal?"

"It has been a while," Yvonne admitted. "I don't want to impose."

"Nonsense." Nita rose from her seat. "I'll whip you up something quick. How about your favorite?"

"All right." Yvonne knew better than to argue with Nita. Yvonne suspected that she herself had gotten her stubbornness from the woman.

Yvonne folded her arms on the table and watched as Nita began gathering the ingredients. Yvonne's 'favorite' dish, a simple Chinese stir-fry made of eggs and tomatoes with rice, hadn't been her favorite since she was a child, but she didn't say that to Nita. For Yvonne, it tasted like her childhood, at least, the good parts of it. She had fond memories of Nita cooking it for her, and of helping Nita cook it when her father wasn't around to disapprove of Yvonne doing something so menial.

Nita opened the fridge and took out a few eggs. "This was your mother's favorite too. She used to eat this when she was pregnant with you. That's probably how you got a taste for it."

Yvonne had vague memories of her mother cooking it, but since Yvonne was only three when her mother died, she didn't know if those memories were even real.

Nita cracked the eggs in a bowl and began scrambling them. "She used to go into the kitchen and cook it at all hours. When she was too far along to be on her feet, I'd cook it for her. I was just one of the maids back then, but since I was the only one on staff who knew how to cook the food she liked, she took me on as her personal maid. That's how I ended up as your nanny."

Nita had told Yvonne this story at least a hundred times, but Yvonne liked hearing it, along with all Nita's other stories of her mother. After her mother's death, it had been like her father had wanted to forget about Yvonne's mother entirely. When he'd remarried, he'd practically erased Yvonne's mother from existence. He hadn't cared about Yvonne keeping any connection to her mother or her culture.

It had been isolating for Yvonne, never having that part of herself acknowledged. If she hadn't had Nita growing up, Yvonne would have been lost. Nita had been close to Yvonne's mother, despite her status as 'the help.' On top of telling Yvonne stories of her mother, Nita had taught Yvonne to cook all her mother's favorite Chinese dishes, and taught her to speak a little Mandarin. Nita had made sure Yvonne knew she had a place, both in the wider world and by her side.

Nita was her family.

Yvonne got up from the table. "Let me help you."

Nita gave her a stern look. "You're my guest. Sit back down."

Yvonne sat. There was no point arguing with her.

Nita began chopping up the tomatoes into small wedges. "So, how's your brother?"

"No idea," Yvonne said. "It's not like we have weekly phone calls."

Nita shook her head. "You should make more of an effort. He's family."

Yvonne scoffed. "Nicholas certainly doesn't consider me family." Before Nita could argue, she changed the subject. "I have some news. Big news."

Nita stopped chopping and looked at her. "What is it?"

Yvonne held up her left hand, brandishing her ring. "I got married."

Nita broke out into a smile. "Congratulations! That's wonderful."

"You're not surprised?"

"I am, but I'm happy for you too. Who's the lucky lady?"

"Her name is Ruby," Yvonne said. "She's… a waitress."

"Do you love her?"

Once again, Yvonne found that she couldn't lie. Not to Nita. "It's more of an arrangement."

"That sounds more like the Yvonne I know."

Surprisingly, Nita didn't question Yvonne about the details of the arrangement, probably because she was used to Yvonne's idiosyncratic behavior. Yvonne wasn't complaining. She didn't want to have to explain that Nita herself was one of the reasons she'd gotten married in the first place.

Nita tossed the eggs into the wok. "Does she make you happy, at least?"

"The jury is still out on that one," Yvonne replied.

"Xiǎo táo." Nita shook her head. "When are you going to start thinking about finding happiness for yourself?"

"I *am* happy."

"That's right. You have your fancy apartment, your high-powered job, and now a pretty wife you have an 'arrangement' with. Is that really all you want from life? We're social creatures. We weren't meant to be alone."

"I'm not alone," Yvonne said. "I have all the friends I need. And I have you."

Nita murmured with disapproval. "That's not the same thing."

"That's enough about me." Yvonne got the same lecture

every time she visited Nita. She'd heard it all before. "What's been going on with you? How are the kids?"

"They're great. Sara is applying for colleges. She has her sights set on some good schools. Her grades should be high enough that she can get some scholarships..." Nita's gaze grew distant. "I don't know what we'll do if she doesn't get them. I don't have the heart to tell her we can't afford to pay a single cent. She doesn't know about everything that's been going on. None of the kids do."

Yvonne felt a sinking in her stomach. Nita's family's problems stemmed from her husband's real estate business. He had invested heavily in the growing local market over the years. Then the market had crashed, and the business had gone into the red. In an attempt to dig it out, Mark had gotten desperate. He'd fallen for shady investment schemes. He'd taken out loan after loan, putting their house up as collateral. He'd stopped paying the taxes he owed. Then, when he'd exhausted conventional lines of credit, he'd turned to dodgy lenders with criminal connections. And now, they were coming to collect.

Nita hadn't told Yvonne about the state of their finances until it was too late. By then, their debts were too large. They owed millions to their creditors, banks, and government agencies, not to mention the shady lenders to whom bankruptcy meant nothing. Nita's family was poised to lose everything within a year.

But Yvonne was going to do something about it. It was why she wanted to get her hands on her inheritance in the first place.

"Nita," Yvonne said. "I already told you, I'll take care of it."

"No." Nita noticed the wok had started to burn. She stirred it. "I couldn't ask that of you. You've already helped us so much. We'll figure this out ourselves."

"Nita, you know this problem is too big for you to solve on your own. I'm not going to sit by and watch you go bankrupt. I'm going to help you."

Nita tried to protest, but Yvonne cut her off. "I've come up with a plan for how to solve your problems once and for all. I'm coming into some money soon. I'll have more than enough money to make this all go away. I'm going to pay off Mark's business debts. I'm going to buy you this house, and I'm going to set up trusts for the kids with money to go toward their education, their futures. Mark *won't* be able to touch them." Nita's husband had proved he couldn't manage money, so that was for the best. "The money needs to go toward your debt and your family futures, not more investments and schemes."

Nita shook her head. "That's too much. You've already given me, given us, so much. I couldn't possibly ask for more."

"Nita, you've done so much for me. You were there for me when no one else was. After my mother passed, you were the only person who kept her memory alive for me. And you were family when my real family wasn't there. After everything you've done for me, I owe you."

Nita turned off the stove and set the wok aside. "You don't owe me anything. Everything I did for you was because I cared about you. Love, relationships, they're not transactions."

"Even so, I'm going to help you."

"That's kind of you, but I can't accept what you're offering."

"I'm not giving you a choice." Yvonne crossed her arms. "If it makes things easier, you can look at it this way. It's not for you, it's for the kids. You want them to have a good future, don't you?"

"Of course."

"Then accept my help. You know it's the right thing to do."

Nita hesitated. "Can I think about it?"

"Take all the time you want. I need some time to get the money together anyway." Yvonne made a mental note to call the executor of her father's estate. She wanted to get on top of everything so she could claim half of the money as soon as the three-month mark hit.

"Thank you." Nita gave her a small smile. "You're so much like your mother. She was a kind and generous soul."

Yvonne suppressed a scoff. 'Kind' was the last word anyone would use to describe her.

Nita finished cooking and dished out the meal, the familiar aroma of the stir-fry filling the air. It tasted even better than it smelled.

Yvonne and Nita spent the next couple of hours catching up. Before they knew it, it was late afternoon.

"I should get started on dinner," Nita said. "Are you staying? Mark and the kids will be back soon, I'm sure they'll be happy to see you."

Yvonne shook her head. "As delicious as your cooking is, I need to get home."

"I wouldn't want to keep you from your new wife. Tell

her I said hello. You'll have to bring her over so I can meet her."

"I will." Yvonne had no intention of doing so. Keeping up appearances was one thing. Having Nita tell Ruby Yvonne's embarrassing childhood stories was another.

"Before I go." Yvonne dug into her purse and pulled out the check she'd written. "The money I gave you would have run out by now. This should tide you over for a while. If you need more to keep the debt collectors at bay, let me know."

Nita held her hands up in front of her defensively. "I can't possibly-"

"Just take it. For the kids."

Nita sighed. "All right." She took the check and folded it up, slipping it into her pocket. "Thank you," she said quietly.

They said their goodbyes, and Yvonne left the house. As she walked to the car, she pulled out her phone. She needed to call the executor of her father's estate to let him know she'd be claiming her inheritance soon.

She unlocked her phone. There was a message from Ruby.

I'm ready to sign the contract.

Finally. The timing couldn't have been better. Ruby didn't know it yet, but she and Yvonne had plans for the night, plans which required Ruby to have signed the contract. But first, Yvonne had to make that phone call.

She sat in her car and dialed the number of Bill Marsden, the executor of her father's estate. Bill was a lawyer and an old family friend. He'd known Yvonne's parents before she was even born. He seemed to like Yvonne, but they weren't particularly close.

When he picked up the phone, Yvonne cut to the chase.

"Bill, it's Yvonne. Yvonne Maxwell. I need to talk to you about my inheritance."

"Yvonne," Bill said. "I haven't heard from you in a long time. How are you?"

"I'm fine." Yvonne skipped the pleasantries. "I got married recently. I want to claim the funds my father left me."

"You're married? Congratulations."

"Thank you." It was a good sign that Bill hadn't already heard about Yvonne's marriage through the grapevine. That meant Yvonne's stepmother and brother likely hadn't heard about it either. She wasn't looking forward to dealing with the fallout of when they inevitably found out. "So, about the inheritance."

"Yes." Bill paused. "It's been a while since I've looked at the terms, but if I remember correctly, you need to be married for some time before you can access the funds."

"That's correct. I can access half the funds at three months, and the other half after a year. I've only been married for a few weeks, but I want to get the ball rolling."

"I'll have to look it up, but I'm sure you're right. I'll need some time to get everything in order. On your end, I'll need you to provide proof that you've met the conditions your father set. You'll need a reliable witness that can attest that your marriage is genuine."

"Yes, I know. That's fine." It was going to be tricky finding a witness, but Yvonne would manage.

"Then I'll set an appointment for ten weeks' time. You'll need to come along with your husband and your witness."

"Wife," Yvonne said.

"Pardon?"

"My wife, not my husband."

"Oh. Yes, your wife." He cleared his throat. "Shall I go ahead and set the appointment?"

"Yes. Thank you."

Before Bill could ask too many questions, Yvonne said a polite goodbye and hung up. She started her car. She needed to get home to Ruby so she could prepare for the night ahead.

CHAPTER 11

Ruby waited for Yvonne to return home, the contract on the table before her, butterflies filling her stomach.

She was ready for this. She'd spent the entire week poring over the contract, thinking hard about her limits and what she wanted. It had been a long, painful week at that. The entire time, Yvonne had continued to hold Ruby at her usual distance. However, once or twice, Ruby had caught Yvonne looking at her in a way that suggested she'd like nothing more than a repeat of that night in Ruby's bedroom.

But it hadn't happened. Instead, Ruby had spent every night replaying in her mind the moment Yvonne came to her door. Ruby had lain awake, fantasizing about all the things Yvonne could do with her, imagining Yvonne ordering her into that bedroom next to hers and using all those toys on her...

Ruby heard the front door open. She snapped out of her

daydream and sat upright. Moments later, Yvonne strode into the room.

"Good evening, Ruby," she said. "You've looked over the contract?"

Ruby nodded. "I've added in my limits and a safeword. There's nothing else I want to discuss." The contract was thorough, covering every detail of their arrangement. Nothing was left unclear.

"Good." Yvonne sat next to Ruby and held out her hand. "Show me."

Ruby handed Yvonne the contract. Yvonne flipped through it, silently examining the sections where Ruby had written things in.

Finally, Yvonne reached the bottom of the final page. She placed the contract on the coffee table. "That all seems to be in order. Do you have any questions or concerns?"

Ruby hesitated. She had zero reservations about what she was agreeing to. However, there was something niggling in the back of her mind. Something she hadn't told Yvonne about.

"Ruby, if there's anything you want to say, now is the time to bring it up," Yvonne said.

Ruby thought for a moment. It wasn't that she'd lied, not really. She'd simply let Yvonne believe something that wasn't quite true about her. And she hadn't told Yvonne about *him*. Ruby knew she should speak up, but she didn't want it to risk their arrangement.

Ruby shook her head. "No. There's nothing I want to say."

Yvonne studied Ruby, her lips pursed. Ruby's heart

thudded against her chest. Could Yvonne see through her lie?

"All right," Yvonne finally said. "I'll type up the amendments and print copies for us both. We can sign them after dinner."

Ruby nodded, relief washing over her. It was like their other contract all over again. Yvonne certainly took everything seriously, and this was no exception.

"Once we've taken care of the contract, there's somewhere I want to take you. Are you free tonight?"

"Yes." It wasn't like Ruby ever had plans. She was still no closer to figuring out what to do with herself and her time.

"Good. We're going out."

Ruby frowned. "Where to?"

"I'm taking you to a private club. It's a place where people go to live out their darkest desires."

What did that mean? Ruby had been to private clubs plenty of times before, but something told her this club wasn't the kind of place where people simply sat around drinking expensive champagne.

"My friends will be there, so we'll get to kill two birds with one stone," Yvonne said. "I get to introduce my new 'wife' to those closest to me, and you'll get a taste of what you so desperately desire."

Ruby nodded. "Okay."

"Wonderful." Yvonne's eyes slid down Ruby's body. "I took the liberty of finding you something to wear. Something appropriate for the venue."

Ruby's skin grew hot. There was that look again, the look that suggested Yvonne was peeling off Ruby's clothes with her eyes.

But as usual, Yvonne didn't act upon her obvious desire. "I'll give it to you once we've signed the contract. We'll head out afterward." Yvonne picked up the contract and rose from the couch. "Until then, I'll be in my study if you need me."

Yvonne left the room. Ruby sighed. Once again, Yvonne had left her hanging.

At least this time, she didn't have to wait much longer.

∽

Ruby and Yvonne pulled up in front of the club. The contract was signed. Ruby was officially Yvonne's submissive.

As her first act as Ruby's Dominant, Yvonne had adorned Ruby in an outfit of her choosing, a dark blue lacy dress that wouldn't have looked out of place at a cocktail party. However, the dress's details hinted at something far more risqué. It was cut low in the front, with straps that crossed over the tops of Ruby's breasts and looped around her neck in a look that was reminiscent of a collar.

Yvonne turned to her. "Ready to go in?"

"Sure," Ruby replied.

They got out of the car. Yvonne straightened out her dress. It was simple compared to Ruby's, black and knee length with three-quarter sleeves, but it fit Yvonne like it had been sewn onto her body.

How did Yvonne manage to make something so plain look so enticing?

As they started down the sidewalk, Yvonne spoke to

Ruby. "My friends and I come here quite often. This is the perfect way to introduce them to you."

"So that's why you brought me here?" Ruby teased. "Not so you can show off your new toy?" Being arm candy for her rich clients was basically half her job.

"I'm not the type who feels the need to show off. Besides." She ran her eyes down Ruby's body. "I prefer to play with my toys in private."

Heat lapped at Ruby's cheeks. Was Yvonne planning to do just that, tonight?

Yvonne reverted to her restrained self. "This is all for the sake of the inheritance. For me to claim the money, we're going to need a witness to the fact that our marriage is real. The more we're seen together, the more convincing this charade is, and the easier that will be. Fooling my friends will be a challenge, but I'm sure you can do it. Just relax and be yourself."

"I've played girlfriend for clients before," Ruby said. "I once went to a party with a woman who wanted to get back at her ex-husband because he cheated on her with a younger woman. Now that was a fun night." Why was Ruby babbling all of a sudden? Was she actually nervous? "Playing wife won't be too different."

Yvonne stopped walking. "Ruby, I don't want you to *play* anything. I don't want you to try to be who you think I want you to be. I want the *real* you."

Ruby nodded. "I can do that."

"Good. We're here."

Ruby looked toward the nondescript black door beside them. Above it was a sign with the words *Lilith's Den* written on it in red flowing script.

Ruby followed Yvonne into a small foyer where Ruby was given several documents to sign. Yvonne explained that the club was highly exclusive, and all members and their guests were vetted and had to sign non-disclosure agreements and waivers. As Ruby skimmed the pages, she resisted the urge to make a joke about how many contracts Yvonne had had her sign over the past few weeks. She had to get her nerves under control.

When Ruby finished signing the paperwork, Yvonne ushered her into the club. Ruby looked around in awe. She'd been to high-class clubs before, but this was something else. For starters, it was far more elegant than the clubs in Vegas.

Plus, there were the more unusual elements. The weird bondage furniture scattered around the room. The fact that while half the crowd was dressed in semi-formal attire, the other half was dressed in leather and corsets. And over in the corner, a woman wearing nothing but a thong was strapped to a cross and being whipped by another woman, while others stood by casually, drinking champagne as they looked on. It confirmed what Ruby had suspected from the moment Yvonne had told her where they were going tonight.

Lilith's Den was a BDSM club.

"This place is something else," Ruby said.

"There's nowhere quite like Lilith's Den," Yvonne said. "It's owned by a friend of mine. If we run into her tonight, I'll introduce you. For now, let's go find the others. They should be at our usual spot."

Ruby followed Yvonne through the crowd, trying not to stare at everything around her. They reached a table near the back of the room. There was only one person there, a wavy-haired brunette with model good looks. She gave Yvonne and Ruby a small wave as they approached.

"Gabrielle," Yvonne said. "This is Ruby. Ruby, this is Gabrielle."

"Hi," Ruby said. Yvonne had filled Ruby in on her friends on the car ride to the club. Gabrielle Hall was one of the women Yvonne owned and ran Mistress Media with. There were five in total.

"It's a pleasure to finally meet you." Gabrielle looked pointedly at Yvonne. "I was beginning to wonder whether you actually existed."

Yvonne ignored the woman's comment and sat down with Ruby. "Are the others here yet?"

"Lydia said she was busy, as usual. Madison and Blair are on their way. Amber is around somewhere." Gabrielle looked over their heads. "Ah, here she is."

Ruby turned to see another woman striding toward them, a tall blonde with an unmistakable air of superiority.

"Yvonne, you're here. And you brought your wife." Amber slid into the seat across from them and crossed her arms. "Well? Are you going to introduce us?"

"Amber, this is Ruby," Yvonne said. "Ruby, Amber."

The woman fit the description Yvonne had given Ruby of Amber to a tee. Amber Pryce was the heiress to the Pryce family. She was the closest thing the country had to royalty. It showed in the way she held herself.

"Nice to meet you," Ruby said.

Amber skimmed her eyes over Ruby, appraising her like she was a piece of antique furniture. "So you're Ruby. I'd tell you 'I've heard so much about you,' but Yvonne hasn't told us a thing. She's been keeping you secret all this time."

"What can I say?" Yvonne took Ruby's hand and drew it into her lap. "I wanted Ruby all to myself."

Ruby's skin tingled at Yvonne's touch. Why was she so jumpy? This was just another pretend girlfriend gig.

A waitress, dressed in a corset and stiletto heels, came over to take their drink orders. As soon as she was gone, Amber sat forward, examining Yvonne and Ruby.

"So," she said. "How did the two of you meet? Yvonne said it was on one of her trips to Vegas."

"I already told you the story," Yvonne said.

"I want to hear it from Ruby. When you talk about the two of you, it's like pulling teeth."

Ruby wasn't surprised that Yvonne had been unconvincing when telling her friends about her 'relationship' with Ruby. Fortunately, Yvonne's friends seemed to think her reluctance when it came to discussing the topic was a personality quirk.

Ruby was a much better actress than Yvonne. And right now, all eyes were on her.

It was time for her to earn her million dollars.

"We met at a bar in Vegas," Ruby began. "I'd just finished work for the night and was having a drink. Yvonne was sitting at the bar by herself, so I went up and talked to her."

"Oh?" Amber's voice was tinged with amusement. "You were the one who made the first move?"

Ruby glanced at 'her wife,' who was struggling to hide her discomfort. "I tried to, but Yvonne made it clear she wasn't having any of it. I had to work hard to win her over." That much was true. It garnered a smirk from Gabrielle. "Then we got talking, had a few drinks, and one thing led to another. Yvonne flew back here the next day, but we kept in touch, and we started seeing each other casually whenever we got the chance."

"And how exactly did you end up married?" Amber asked.

"Well, over time, things between us became less casual. Over time, we realized we had serious feelings for each other." Ruby gazed lovingly at Yvonne for effect. "That was when we decided to tie the knot. It just felt right at the time."

Ruby glanced at Amber and Gabrielle. It was clear they weren't convinced.

"Okay, honestly?" Ruby said. "We were both completely drunk when we decided to get married. But once we woke up the next morning, we talked about our feelings and decided we wanted to stay married. We both wanted to be together, but we hadn't had the courage to do anything about it until that night. The feelings had always been there."

This time, when Ruby looked at the other women, they were studying Yvonne, who had managed to maintain her usual inscrutable expression throughout Ruby's story. Nerves flitted in Ruby's stomach. Could everyone see through the ruse?

After what felt like forever, Amber finally spoke. "I'm happy for the two of you." She leaned back and crossed her legs. "And I'm glad you've found love, Yvonne."

"I'm happy for you too," Gabrielle said.

"Thank you," Yvonne said.

As the waitress returned with their drinks, Yvonne pulled her phone out of her purse, frowning.

"Madison's calling me. I should take this somewhere

quieter." She looked at Ruby, wariness flickering behind her eyes. "Do you mind?"

"Go ahead." Ruby didn't exactly want to be left alone with Yvonne's prying friends, but what choice did she have?

"I'll be right back." Yvonne gave Ruby's leg an affectionate pat. Was this Yvonne attempting to behave like they were newlyweds, madly in love? At the very least, it was in character for Yvonne. Ruby couldn't imagine that Yvonne was big on public displays of affection, even with a real partner.

As soon as Yvonne left, Gabrielle looked at her, a sly smile on her face.

"So," Gabrielle said. "You're Yvonne's wife."

Ruby nodded. She wasn't sure what else to say.

Gabrielle examined Ruby intently. "Why hasn't she ever mentioned you?"

Ruby swallowed. "I-"

"Gabi," Amber warned. "You're making the poor thing uncomfortable."

"I'm just curious about this woman who has melted Yvonne's heart," Gabrielle said. "You have to admit, this is unexpected."

Amber scoffed dismissively. "The marriage? Yes. The fact that Yvonne had a secret girlfriend? Not so much. She's not the type to shout this kind of thing from the rooftops."

"I suppose you're right. It would explain a lot. In all the time I've known her, I don't remember Yvonne ever having a girlfriend. Lovers, yes, but that was all. Perhaps it's because she's been secretly pining over you this whole time." Gabrielle swirled her drink in her glass and sipped it slowly. "I always suspected she had a heart under there, despite her ice-cold bitch act." She looked at Ruby. "No offense toward your wife intended."

"None taken." Ruby smiled. "Why do you think I married her? I like that about her."

Gabrielle's mouth curled up at one side. "This is all starting to make sense. It seems Yvonne found someone who's happy to put up with her demanding ways."

Amber gave her a disapproving look. "Be nice, Gabi."

"What?" Gabrielle said. "It's true. We all know how Yvonne is. I like a little power exchange as much as any other Domme, but Yvonne takes it all so seriously. Where's the fun in that?"

Ruby's stomach flipped. What exactly had she gotten herself into? Was she going to regret signing that contract?

She decided to change the subject. "So, how do you know Yvonne? You all run Mistress together?"

"Yes, but we were friends before that," Gabrielle said. "We spend a lot of time here, actually. It's how we got to know each other."

That explained a lot. Ruby had been starting to wonder if there was something in the water over at Mistress Media that had all their execs hanging out at a BDSM club just for fun.

Before Ruby could question them further, Yvonne returned, taking a seat next to her.

"Madison and Blair got caught up with some kind of wedding emergency, but they're on their way." She slipped her hand into Ruby's. "Is everything okay here?"

Was Yvonne worried that Gabrielle and Amber had interrogated Ruby in her absence? Ruby gave her a reassuring smile. "Everything is great."

Gabrielle and Amber picked up where they left off, grilling Yvonne and Ruby about their relationship. They were soon joined by Gabrielle's girlfriend, Dana, as well as Madison and her fiancée, Blair. After a flurry of introductions, Ruby found herself fielding an endless stream of questions about herself and Yvonne.

When the conversation finally moved on, Yvonne spoke quietly to Ruby. "Enjoying yourself?"

Ruby nodded. "I am."

"And what do you think of this place?"

Ruby glanced around the room. Nearby, there was a woman in a cage while another woman sat casually on top of it. "It's... intriguing." It wasn't just the club that intrigued Ruby. This whole world Yvonne inhabited—one of glamour and luxury, pleasure and power games—was exhilarating.

"What you see before you is only the tip of the iceberg. There's so much more to Lilith's Den than what's down here." Yvonne glanced toward the others, then back to Ruby, a dangerously sexy look in her eyes. "We're going to play nice for everyone for a little while longer. Then I'm going to give you a taste of what you've been begging me for."

CHAPTER 12

After a couple of hours, the others slowly dispersed, leaving Yvonne and Ruby alone.

"It's time I showed you the real reason I brought you here." Yvonne rose from her seat, beckoning Ruby to follow. "Come with me."

Ruby followed Yvonne toward the back of the club, drawing more than a few glances as they passed through the crowd. Ruby couldn't help but notice that every time someone's eyes fell upon her, as soon as they spotted Yvonne with her, they would look away. Was it that obvious that Yvonne was Ruby's Mistress? Was it that obvious that Ruby belonged to her?

They reached a set of doors which were guarded by a bouncer. Yvonne flashed a key, and the bouncer waved them through.

They continued up some stairs to find a long hallway with an endless number of doors at either side. Yvonne walked purposefully toward one of them and unlocked it with the key.

"Go on in," she said.

Ruby stepped through the door and looked around the room. It was plain and bare, with only a couple of wooden chairs and a scattering of cushions on the floor as furniture. There were a series of wooden beams along the ceiling, low enough for a person to reach up and touch. The wall at the far end of the room was covered with a seamless mirror, and on all the other walls were tasteful, artsy photographs of nude women bound up in ropes.

Heat rose to Ruby's skin at the sight. "What is this place?"

"This is The Rope Room," Yvonne replied.

Ruby looked at one of the photographs closely. The woman in it lay on a sea of silk, red ropes encircling her body in intricate patterns. In the photo next to it, a woman appeared to be suspended from something above the photo, hanging sideways in midair with her limbs bound together, wrapped in a cocoon of ropes.

Yvonne spoke from beside Ruby, startling her. "They're beautiful, aren't they?"

"It's almost like they're caught in webs." Ruby glanced up at the beams above them. "Is that what you're going to do to me?"

"I'm not going to suspend you up from the ceiling. At least, not tonight." Yvonne drew the back of her fingers down the side of Ruby's cheek. "Consider this an introduction. A taste of all the delights to come."

A shiver rippled down Ruby's neck. She'd been worried that when faced with the reality of Yvonne's twisted desires, she'd find herself overwhelmed, just as Yvonne had warned her. And considering everything that had happened with her last client, all this should have scared her.

But instead, the hunger inside her grew.

"Well?" Yvonne said. "How would you like to get caught in my web?"

Ruby gazed back at her, unable to do anything but nod. She was already caught in Yvonne's web.

"Then let's get you out of that dress."

Yvonne took the hem of Ruby's dress and drew it up and over Ruby's head. She wasn't wearing a bra underneath, so she was left in nothing but her panties. Yvonne's eyes skimmed Ruby's body approvingly, sending warmth creeping up Ruby's cheeks. Yvonne showed no sign of stripping down herself. Ruby suspected Yvonne preferred it that way.

Silence filled the air, the club downstairs a world away. Yvonne guided Ruby to the center of the room to stand underneath one of the wooden beams, then opened a cupboard and withdrew several coils of rope.

Yvonne placed all but one of them down on a nearby chair, then took Ruby's wrists and bound them together firmly, leaving a tail of rope dangling from them. Lifting Ruby's arms above her head, Yvonne tied the rope to the beam above her. Ruby resisted the urge to tug on her bonds. She was certain Yvonne would see it as a sign of disobedience. And if Yvonne had made anything clear, it was that she required Ruby's complete obedience.

Yvonne wound the tail of the rope around Ruby's arms, binding them together tightly in a series of knots. She continued down Ruby's shoulders, then wound the rope around Ruby's chest and back, crossing it over and under and between her breasts. The rope was surprisingly soft, caressing her skin in a not unpleasant way.

Yvonne took a step back, surveying her work. While Ruby's bonds weren't tight enough to constrict, the firm pressure of the ropes felt immobilizing. The ropes were all connected, so the slightest movement of her body made them tighten and shift in the most delicious way.

Yvonne took the waist of Ruby's panties and stripped them down her legs, leaving her naked and exposed. Ruby's heart raced.

Yvonne trailed her hand down the center of Ruby's stomach. "I'm not done with you yet. Spread your feet apart."

Ruby obeyed. Yvonne took the rope hanging from Ruby's chest, slipped it between Ruby's thighs, and pulled it up at the back, tying it off between her shoulder blades. The slight pressure of the rope between Ruby's legs made the urge to move unbearable. Ruby shifted her hips, causing the rope to rub against her. She let out a surprised gasp, a dart of pleasure shooting deep into her.

Yvonne's lips curled up at the corners. "That should encourage you to stay still while I finish tying you up."

Ruby stopped moving, but it didn't help. Even breathing made the rope shift, nudging against her most sensitive places, amplifying the heat within her with every second. All the while, Yvonne continued, tying the ropes down Ruby's stomach, hips, and thighs, all the way to her ankles.

"Now I'm finished." Yvonne drew her eyes down Ruby's bound body. "What a tantalizing work of art you are." She stepped to the side, giving Ruby a clear view of herself in the mirror. "Take a look for yourself?"

Ruby looked at herself in the mirror. She was bound from head to toe, a ladder of knots running down the front of her body, from her upstretched arms, to her hips, then down each of her legs.

She drew in a breath. She certainly felt like a piece of art, living and breathing. The contrast between the dark ropes and her skin was striking, and restrained as she was, Ruby was as helpless as a sculpture. Although her legs were free, with her arms stretched high above her, she could barely move.

Yvonne watched Ruby in the mirror, a ravenous look in her eyes. "Think about all the things I could do with you right now."

She drew her palm down Ruby's chest, sweeping it over her breast. Ruby's breathing deepened, causing the rope between her legs to pull, sending ripples of need through her. A whimper fell from her lips.

"By the looks of things, I don't even have to do anything," Yvonne said. "I could simply leave you as you are and watch you slowly come undone."

Ruby bit back a groan. She was quickly reaching the point where her arousal was becoming unbearable, and Yvonne had barely touched her. This was all Ruby's own doing, yet she was unable to relieve the ache within herself.

Yvonne stepped in close, pressing her body to Ruby's, letting her lips graze Ruby's cheek. "But what's the fun of having a toy when you can't play with her?"

She reached down their bodies and tugged the rope running between Ruby's thighs upward. Ruby gasped, pleasure reverberating through her. Yvonne ran her hand up Ruby's chest, tweaking a nipple with her fingertips.

Ruby bucked against Yvonne. She was already right on the edge.

And it was clear Yvonne knew it. "I'm not letting you come yet. Didn't I tell you that your pleasure is mine to give?"

"Yes," Ruby murmured.

"Do you think you've earned the privilege of pleasure?"

Ruby hesitated. "No, Mistress."

"Are you saying that because you know it's what I want to hear?"

Ruby lowered her gaze. "Yes, Mistress."

Yvonne let out a soft, velvety chuckle. "I appreciate your honesty. And I'm a merciful Mistress. You'll get your release, but on my terms, not yours."

Yvonne took the rope running down the center of Ruby's body and pulled it aside so it was no longer between Ruby's nether lips. She let a hand roam down the front of Ruby's body, skimming over her bare stomach, slipping down the inside of her thigh. Ruby pulsed with anticipation.

Yvonne leaned close, drawing her thumb down Ruby's lower lip. "From the moment I tasted these lips of yours, I've been dying to find something out." She traced her fingers up Ruby's slick slit. "Does the rest of you taste as sweet?"

Ruby blew out a hard, sharp breath. Yvonne drew her lips down Ruby's neck, leaving a wet trail behind. She continued downward slowly, painting them over Ruby's breasts and nipples, all the way to her belly button. Ruby shuddered, Yvonne's wet lips soothing her burning skin.

Yvonne looked up at her, her dark eyes alight. "This is the only time you'll ever see me on my knees."

Yvonne knelt, her breath searing Ruby's inner thighs. Ruby trembled. Yvonne's lips wandered up to where Ruby's thighs met, her touch featherlight, and drew her tongue over Ruby's folds. Ruby groaned softly, her hips pushing out toward the other woman, straining her bonds to their limits. But Yvonne only drew back an equal amount. There was no rushing her.

So Ruby closed her eyes and wrapped her fingers around the rope above her head, giving in to the sweet torment. The more Ruby relaxed, the more Yvonne rewarded her, her touch growing firmer and more deliberate. She pursed her lips around Ruby's clit, sucking gently. She teased Ruby's entrance with her tongue. She grabbed onto Ruby's ass cheeks, holding tightly as she devoured Ruby. Ruby slackened in her bonds, purring from her chest as she slipped into a trance of bliss.

It didn't take long for her pleasure to peak. Her head flew back, her body quaking as an explosion of ecstasy tore through her. It faded just as quickly as it came. But Yvonne continued, her mouth working at the peak of Ruby's thighs, more gently now, but still unhesitating. In her bound, blissdrunk state, Ruby was powerless against her. Not that she wanted Yvonne to stop. Although Yvonne was unrelenting, her mouth, her lips, her tongue, felt so exquisite.

"Oh, god!" Ruby stiffened as another climax gripped her, just as intense as the last, but it drew on and on until Ruby felt like her body had been sucked dry.

She let out a long, slow breath. Yvonne rose to her feet again, cupped Ruby's cheeks and kissed her hard and deep, sucking the air from her chest. Ruby's head spun. She could taste herself on Yvonne's lips.

Yvonne drew back, a hint of amusement in her eyes. "I have to say, I'm disappointed. That was over far too soon. I was planning to toy with you at least another hour."

Ruby barely heard her. She was lost in a trance, deep under her Mistress's spell.

"But I wouldn't want such a willing, eager captive to go to waste." Yvonne took another coil of rope from the chair next to her, drawing it through her fingers. "I'm going to take this opportunity to show you all my favorite ties. Would you like that? If you're good, I might even give you another reward."

"Yes, Mistress," Ruby murmured. Despite her exhaustion, she still wanted more.

A smile crossed Yvonne's lips. "You're a greedy little thing, aren't you?" She brushed a stray strand of hair out of Ruby's face. "I'm going to enjoy this."

As Yvonne unfurled the coil of rope, a thought floated into Ruby's hazy mind.

If this was Yvonne's idea of giving Ruby 'a taste,' what else did Yvonne have in store for her?

∽

When they returned home, Yvonne practically had to carry Ruby from the car up to the apartment. She clung to Yvonne's proffered arm like she was in a drunken haze.

Yvonne knew exactly what Ruby was going through. It was a high, a feeling of euphoria submissives experienced, caused by all the adrenaline and endorphins the body produced in response to intense physical stimulus.

Yvonne steered Ruby into her bedroom. "Get into bed. Get undressed first. I'll get you some water."

Ruby nodded and sat on the bed, slipping out of her heels.

Yvonne left Ruby's bedroom and went into the kitchen. She leaned back against the counter, taking a moment for herself. It had surprised Yvonne, how quickly and deeply Ruby had slipped into that submissive headspace, how easily she'd let go. Clearly, Yvonne's initial impression of her had been wrong. Ruby wasn't simply trying to please Yvonne. Her desire to submit was something innate.

And that made Yvonne uneasy.

She didn't quite understand why. Was she worried Ruby wouldn't respect her own limits, that she would push herself too far? That was a risk for new submissives. But Yvonne had stressed the importance of being honest with herself and Yvonne about what she could handle, and Ruby seemed to understand. Besides, Yvonne was experienced enough that she would never push Ruby too hard. She had every intention of taking things slow and treating Ruby with a careful hand.

So why did Yvonne feel this irrational level of concern for her?

Yvonne poured a glass of water, then returned to Ruby's bedroom. Ruby was already in bed.

"Here." She handed the glass to Ruby. "Drink this, or you'll feel terrible in the morning."

Ruby did as she was told. Yvonne took the empty glass from her and set it on the nightstand, then sat down on the edge of the bed.

"How are you feeling?" she asked. "Is there anything else you need?"

"No, I'm good," Ruby replied.

"I'll stay here until you fall asleep, just to make sure you're all right."

Ruby looked at her curiously. "That's sweet of you."

"I'm just doing my job. You're my submissive. It's my responsibility to look after you."

Ruby rolled her eyes. "Right. Because everything is just 'business' to you."

"I didn't mean-"

"Relax, I'm just teasing you. But honestly, you don't have to fuss over me like this."

"Yes, I do. What we're doing together, it involves a certain level of vulnerability. That state, it leads to all kinds of good feelings. But sometimes, negative feelings surface in their wake, leading to a drop, physically, mentally, emotionally-" Yvonne looked down at Ruby. She had a distant look in her eye and was clearly on the verge of sleep. Now wasn't the time for BDSM 101. "As your Domme, I need to take care of you and make sure all your needs are met in order to prevent that drop. It's simple aftercare."

Ruby gazed up at Yvonne, her thick eyelashes fluttering. "Now that I think about it, there is something you can do for me."

"What is it?"

Ruby hesitated. "Can you get into bed with me?"

Yvonne wasn't surprised by Ruby's request. Physical intimacy was an important part of aftercare. She could leave after Ruby fell asleep. "All right."

She slid into the bed next to Ruby. Ruby settled against her, her back to Yvonne.

Tentatively, Yvonne wrapped an arm around Ruby, drawing her in close. "How's this?"

"This is good." Ruby peered back at her, smiling. "I'm feeling better already."

Ruby grabbed the sheets and pulled them up over them, letting out a contented sigh. The room lapsed into silence. The scent of Ruby's hair filled Yvonne's head. It was something sweet and light.

Yvonne spoke quietly. "Ruby?"

"Mmhm?"

"Thank you for tonight, with my friends. They can be... a lot."

"It's no problem. I had fun." Ruby turned to face her. "I hope I made a good impression."

"You did. You were perfect. You seemed comfortable. Genuine."

"I tried to do what you said. To be myself." Ruby's voice faltered. "But it was hard. I've spent so long being who people want me to be. Who clients want me to be..."

Yvonne examined her. The distant, unfocused look in Ruby's eyes suggested she was still in a vulnerable headspace.

She stroked Ruby's arm reassuringly. "You don't have to do that anymore. Not for me. You can just be yourself. I want the real you, Ruby."

Ruby was silent for a moment. "It's just that, sometimes, I feel like I don't even remember who the real me is."

"And now is the perfect time for you to try to figure that out. You have a whole year of no obligations. No clients to please, no expectations. You should take advantage of that. Do things for yourself, things that make you happy. You have unlimited time at your disposal, not to mention money. I checked the statement for that credit card I gave you. You haven't bought anything for yourself other than food and clothes."

"What else am I supposed to buy?"

"Anything. Whatever you want."

Ruby sighed. "I guess I'll have to figure out what that is."

She closed her eyes. Yvonne watched and listened as Ruby's breaths grew slow and deep. After a few minutes, Yvonne got up from the bed, taking care not to disturb Ruby. Ruby didn't stir. She was asleep.

Yvonne lingered at Ruby's bedside, that feeling of concern she'd felt earlier striking her again. At the back of her mind, a voice whispered a single word.

Stay.

But that wasn't an option. Yvonne couldn't afford to get too attached to Ruby.

She slipped out of Ruby's bedroom and shut the door behind her.

CHAPTER 13

Ruby wandered through the department store, her arms saddled with bags. She'd been shopping all morning and half the afternoon, with the intention of buying something for herself. Once again, she'd ended up with nothing other than more clothes and shoes.

Her feet ached, and she couldn't carry anything more. She was ready to go home. But she still hadn't found what she was looking for. The problem?

She didn't know what she was looking for.

She'd said as much to Yvonne that night. Ruby didn't know who she was. She didn't know what she wanted. She'd almost confessed the truth to Yvonne, about *him*, about who he'd been to Ruby, about everything he'd done. About how she'd gotten so used to becoming who he'd wanted her to be that she'd lost all sense of herself, of her identity.

In hindsight, she could see that it had been her way of coping with her situation. It had been easier just to be compliant, to do and say and be whatever he wanted. Ruby had always been the type of person who thrived on pleasing others on some level. He had taken advantage of that.

But that was all in the past. Now, Ruby had the opportunity to find herself again. She needed to figure out how to do that.

And buying another pair of shoes wasn't the answer.

She sighed. It said something about Ruby that it was only because of Yvonne's encouragement that she'd finally decided to figure out what she wanted. Here Ruby was, under someone else's control again. But Yvonne was different. Despite her thirst for control, she wasn't controlling. Whether they were in the bedroom or otherwise, Yvonne would provide Ruby with direction while allowing her to choose whether to follow it. In becoming Ruby's Mistress, Yvonne had given Ruby a sense of stability that she hadn't even known she'd needed. Yvonne was helping Ruby find her way, without even knowing she was doing so.

It made Ruby all the more determined to ensure she was holding up her end of the bargain, both as Yvonne's 'wife' and as her submissive. But Ruby wasn't sure what that entailed. What could someone like Yvonne possibly want? What did she need? The woman was a mystery.

Ruby stopped in the middle of the aisle and looked around her. She'd been wandering aimlessly in the maze of the department store for what felt like hours now, and she was lost. Somehow, she'd ended up in the kitchenware section. Ruby didn't need any kitchenware. She didn't even cook. Why would she cook when she could order a chef-prepared meal from a fancy restaurant every night on Yvonne's dime?

As she tried to get her bearings, Ruby's eyes landed on a

display in the aisle. In the middle was a shiny red stand mixer. She wandered over to it, drawn by a sense of familiarity. The mixer almost looked like one her mother had had in the kitchen growing up, although this one was higher tech.

Suddenly, a memory came back to Ruby. She'd been eight years old, attempting to bake cookies for the first time. She'd had no idea what she was doing, and she'd immediately broken the stand mixer. After her mother had found out, she'd scolded Ruby for a solid ten minutes before taking her hand and teaching her how to bake cookies properly, from start to finish.

That single incident sparked her love of baking. Ruby grew up harboring a silly little dream of opening her own bakery, so she could share her creations with the world. That was what Ruby had loved the most about baking. For her, it was about making and sharing something that came from the heart, something real and genuine, complete with imperfections and flaws.

When had Ruby lost that love? It was one of those frivolous activities that she'd just lost interest in over time. No, that wasn't true. She'd stopped baking because *he* had never approved of it. He'd never approved of her doing anything that didn't serve his interests. He had snuffed out all Ruby's wants and desires in favor of his own.

Ruby stared at the shiny red mixer intently. She knew exactly what she wanted to buy.

∽

The timer on the oven dinged. Ruby opened it up and

pulled out the tray of blueberry muffins, placing it on the counter next to the others. This batch looked a little overcooked, but it was better than her last attempts. It had been years since she'd done any baking, but she was slowly getting back into the rhythm of the process.

"What is going on here?"

Ruby jumped. Yvonne was standing in the doorway to the kitchen, her arms crossed.

"Yvonne," Ruby said. "You're home early." It was barely 6 p.m. Yvonne was usually still at work for another hour or two.

Yvonne's disapproving eyes swept around the room. "Why does my kitchen look like it's been hit by a tornado?"

Her description of the state of the kitchen was accurate. The counters were covered in flour, the sink filled with pans, utensils scattered everywhere. Plus, a shiny new stand mixer took up half the counter. Ruby had planned to clean everything up before Yvonne got home.

"Well, I was thinking about what you said the other night," Ruby began. "About doing something for myself. I wasn't sure where to start, so I went shopping, and while I was out, I remembered that I used to like to bake. So I decided I wanted to do some baking, but you don't own any baking stuff, so I bought some."

She looked at Yvonne. Yvonne was staring back at her, the irritation in her eyes replaced by amusement.

Ruby folded her arms across her chest. "You told me I could buy whatever I wanted."

"I did." Yvonne picked up a stray spatula. "And I meant it. But I tell you that you can buy anything, and you buy kitchen utensils?"

Ruby shrugged. "They're very expensive utensils." That stand mixer had cost a small fortune, but Yvonne was paying for it.

"I didn't take you for the domestic type."

"I'm not. I can't cook to save my life, but baking is different. I'm not going to win any competitions, but I enjoy it. Plus, it gives me a way to kill time while you're at work."

"Oh?" Yvonne raised an eyebrow, her voice lowering. "So you've been sitting around every day, waiting for your Mistress to return home?"

Blood rushed up Ruby's face. "I meant that I need more things to fill my days, that's all."

Yvonne stepped in close. Ruby found herself backed against the counter, the other woman's hands at either side of her. Desire flickered deep within her.

"That's disappointing," Yvonne purred. "I think I like the idea of you waiting for me all day like a good little housewife, longing for me to come through the front door and fuck you right here in the kitchen."

Ruby trembled. The heat between the two of them had only strengthened since that night at Lilith's Den. It was as if Yvonne had finally stopped fighting the attraction she'd had toward Ruby from the moment they had met. This unrestrained side of Yvonne was even more intoxicating.

Yvonne brought her thumb up to stroke Ruby's lip. A wave of lust washed over her.

"So," Yvonne said. "How about a taste?"

Before Ruby could react, Yvonne reached around to grab one of the muffins. Reflexively, Ruby swatted Yvonne's hand away from the hot muffin tin.

Yvonne's mouth fell open. "Did you just slap me?"

Ruby grimaced. "Sorry! Those are too hot to eat."

Yvonne didn't respond, but the dark expression on her face made her annoyance clear.

Crap. "I didn't mean to. My brothers, they were always trying to steal things I'd bake before they were cool. It was a reflex, I swear."

"I am *not* one of your brothers," Yvonne said firmly. "That's no way to treat your Mistress."

Ruby's heart began to race. Despite Yvonne's sharp tone, Ruby could feel the desire radiating from every inch of the other woman's skin. She looked into Yvonne's eyes and found a storm raging behind them wasn't at all due to irritation.

"I'm sorry, Mistress," Ruby said softly.

Yvonne took Ruby's chin in her fingers. "I'm not sure I believe you."

Heat suffused Ruby's body. What did Yvonne want? Ruby to grovel at her feet? She'd already done that once before.

"You have two choices," Yvonne said. "You can write me a long, detailed letter, explaining just how sorry you are." She paused. "Or, you can accept a more physical punishment."

Ruby hesitated. "What do you mean by 'physical?'"

Yvonne's gaze flicked over to the utensils scattered on the counter, a spatula and some mixing spoons.

Ruby's eyes widened. Did Yvonne mean what she thought she did? Ruby had enthusiastically signed up for doing all kinds of kinky things with Yvonne, but this wasn't what she'd had in mind.

Yet, Ruby found the idea hot as hell.

"So," Yvonne said. "Which do you choose?"

Ruby sucked her lip thoughtfully. "The second one."

Ruby didn't miss the smile that flickered across Yvonne's lips. "Good choice."

She picked up a wooden spoon from the counter and flicked it against her hand experimentally, before tossing it aside. "We can do better than this." Yvonne scanned the rest of the utensils before selecting a silicone spatula. She slapped it against her palm. "Yes, this is perfect. Now, do you remember your safeword?"

Ruby nodded.

"Good. Bend over the counter."

Ruby blinked. "You want me to-"

"I wasn't asking."

Ruby took a deep breath and bent over, resting her forearms on the flour-covered countertop, bringing her safeword to the front of her mind. She felt Yvonne's hand at the back of her knee, gliding slowly up the back of her thigh, dragging her skirt up in the process. A shiver went through her, all thoughts of using her safeword gone.

Yvonne pulled the skirt all the way up around Ruby's waist, grazing her hands over Ruby's panty-covered ass cheeks. She drew the spatula along the center of Ruby's back, sending heat rising within her.

"You'd think that something hard and firm would be the best tool for this kind of discipline," Yvonne said. "But it's the more flexible materials that have the most bite."

Yvonne slithered the spatula down to Ruby's ass cheek. Ruby screwed her eyes shut just in time to feel a firm slap on her ass. She gasped, the impact resonating through her, jolting her entire body forward. But in the wake of the pain, Ruby began to burn all over.

Yvonne spanked Ruby again and again, increasing the force with each swat. Ruby sucked in a hard breath. Yvonne had been right about one thing. The innocent-looking spatula packed a punch. Each hit was a sharp sting that diffused along every inch of Ruby's skin until her entire body was afire. A moan escaped Ruby's lips. She buried her head in her arms, her knees threatening to collapse. Yvonne continued to spank her, not holding back any longer, each strike penetrating deeper into her.

Ruby whimpered, the ache within her growing unbearable. Yvonne put the spatula down beside Ruby's head and drew her hand up the back of Ruby's leg.

"Learned your lesson yet?" Yvonne asked.

"Yes," Ruby murmured.

"I don't think you have." Yvonne's hand crept upward toward the inside of Ruby's thigh. "In fact, I think you enjoyed it."

Ruby quivered as Yvonne's hand reached the peak of Ruby's thighs, her fingertips brushing against Ruby's now damp panties.

"Well?" Yvonne pressed her fingers firmly between Ruby's lower lips, sliding them up and down. "Did you enjoy that?"

Ruby nodded, then realized Yvonne couldn't see her head. "Yes. Yes, Mistress."

"Of course you did. I knew you would." Yvonne leaned down over her, her warm breath cradling the back of Ruby's ear. "Your Mistress knows exactly what she's doing."

Ruby exhaled softly. She felt Yvonne pressing against her

ass, her breasts against Ruby's back, pushing her down onto the countertop. Yvonne slid her hands up to Ruby's waist. Ruby let out a breath, desperate for Yvonne to take her there and then, to relieve the throbbing inside her.

Instead, Yvonne took Ruby's skirt and pulled it back down to cover Ruby's legs.

She pulled away. "I'm going to take a shower. I expect the kitchen to be clean when I'm done."

Huh? Ruby straightened up and turned around.

But Yvonne was already gone.

Ruby groaned into the empty kitchen. Was Yvonne serious? Was she really going to leave Ruby like this? She sighed.

Your Mistress knows exactly what she's doing.

∽

When Yvonne finished showering, she headed into the living room to find Ruby waiting for her.

Ruby got up from the couch expectantly. "I've finished cleaning the kitchen."

"Good." Yvonne sat down and grabbed the book she'd left on the coffee table, opening it up.

Ruby hovered by the couch. "So, what are we doing for the rest of the night?"

Yvonne didn't take her eyes off her book. "I don't know about you, but I plan to catch up on some reading."

"Really? That's all?"

"Yes, that's all." Yvonne rarely had the time to read, but she found herself struck with the urge to spend some time relaxing.

Plus, she wanted to toy with Ruby for a few hours.

Ruby let out a skeptical murmur. Yvonne ignored her. After a few seconds, Ruby sat down next to Yvonne. Without thinking, Yvonne glanced up at her.

That was a mistake. Ruby peered back at Yvonne from under her long, thick eyelashes, her blonde hair now loose around her shoulders, one bare, slender leg crossed over the other. She had a smudge of flour on her cheek, and her blue eyes shimmered with lust.

Yvonne's resolve wavered. In the time since they'd met, Ruby had only gotten better at getting under Yvonne's skin. Yvonne looked back down at her book and turned a page carefully, somehow managing to maintain her composure.

"Yvonne?" When Yvonne didn't respond, Ruby pulled down the top of Yvonne's book. "Don't you want to finish what you started in the kitchen?"

Yvonne looked up at her sharply. "Are you questioning your Mistress?"

"No, I just-"

"Let me be clear. What happened in the kitchen wasn't your punishment."

Ruby frowned. "What's that supposed to mean?"

"You'll understand soon enough." Yvonne pulled the book back out of Ruby's fingers.

"Come on," Ruby said. "You're home early, for once. We have the rest of the evening ahead of us. Isn't there something you'd rather be doing?" She traced her fingers up Yvonne's knee, a playful look in her eyes. "Or someone?"

Yvonne put her book down, ignoring the desire Ruby's voice provoked in her. She'd only intended to keep Ruby hanging for a few hours before giving her what she wanted.

But here Ruby was, blatantly trying to steal back control.

Yvonne locked her eyes on Ruby's. "What did I tell you about trying to tempt me? Trying to get me to do what you want?"

Ruby withdrew her hand. "That if I did it again, you'd do far worse than make me crawl."

"And what are you doing right now?"

Ruby lowered her gaze, a gesture of contrition that was entirely unconvincing. "Trying to get you to do what I want."

"If you don't stop, your punishment will only last longer. Don't play games with me, Ruby. You won't win."

Ruby crossed her arms and sat back in the chair, but didn't say anything. As Yvonne began to read again, Ruby glanced back at her, her expression becoming more and more agitated.

But Yvonne only ignored her, until finally, Ruby let out a huff and strode out of the room.

When Yvonne heard Ruby's bedroom door shut, she put down her book and stretched out on the couch. She wasn't the type to play games with her submissive, but she needed to keep Ruby in line without extinguishing the woman's playful side entirely. It was becoming more and more clear that it was a genuine part of Ruby's personality. The last thing Yvonne wanted was to discourage Ruby from expressing herself, especially not now that Ruby was finally letting that mask of hers slip, letting Yvonne see through to the real woman behind it.

Yvonne liked what she saw. She'd thought that Ruby had engineered herself to appeal to Yvonne's fantasies, to be her perfect woman. However, the real Ruby was even more appealing to Yvonne than the woman she'd met at the bar that night. The Ruby who was completely unaware of the flour on her cheek was so much more beautiful. The Ruby who didn't hesitate to express her true desires was so much more irresistible. The woman who had asked Yvonne to get into bed with her that night after they'd returned from Lilith's Den stirred far more inside Yvonne than that seductress who had approached Yvonne at the bar in Vegas.

Was Yvonne getting too attached to Ruby? That was *not* a good idea. Their arrangement was just temporary, and Yvonne had essentially hired Ruby. She had no interest in anything more than physical with the woman. She'd already crossed a line by taking Ruby on as a submissive.

She couldn't let the lines blur any further.

CHAPTER 14

"Hi, Yvonne." Ruby stretched herself out on the couch, peering up at the other woman. "When did you get home?"

Yvonne's gaze skipped along Ruby's body. "What are you wearing?"

"You mean this?"

Although it was still early in the night, Ruby was dressed in what could barely be described as sleepwear. The low-cut satin nightie was a deep red color and had a bow at the front. It was barely long enough to cover the matching panties underneath it. Ruby didn't normally dress so provocatively at home. Most of the time, she wore casual but classy designer outfits in an attempt to dress in a way that was 'befitting of her status' as Yvonne Maxwell's wife. But right now, Ruby was trying to catch her 'wife's' attention.

And the look on Yvonne's face told Ruby it was working.

"I went shopping again today," Ruby said. "I picked up

some new clothes. You told me to buy whatever I wanted. This is something I want."

"That's why you're lying around in practically nothing?" Yvonne scoffed. "I think you have an ulterior motive. I think you're trying to make me end your punishment."

"I'm just doing what you told me to. If my outfit is distracting you, that's not my fault."

Yvonne gave Ruby a sharp look. "Careful. I don't want to have to spank you again."

Ruby flushed. "I didn't mind that. It was everything that came afterward."

Yvonne had told Ruby that the spanking in the kitchen wasn't Ruby's real punishment. It hadn't taken Ruby long to figure out what her real punishment was.

Since that night over a week ago, Yvonne hadn't so much as touched her.

It wasn't the kind of torture Ruby had expected when she'd signed that second contract with Yvonne, but it was torture nonetheless. Ruby had spent the entire week in a state of constant frustration. Every time she'd walked into the kitchen, she'd found herself reliving that moment when Yvonne had had her bent over the counter over and over. And she might have been imagining it, but Yvonne seemed to be playing games with her too. Every time Ruby was in the kitchen with Yvonne, Yvonne would get awfully close, ostensibly to grab something nearby. Whenever they passed each other in the hall, Yvonne would brush against her. And several times a day, Yvonne would summon Ruby to her, as though she intended to finally put an end to her game, but instead, she'd simply ask Ruby an unnecessary question before dismissing her.

It was driving Ruby mad.

"While we're on the topic," Yvonne said. "I've been doing some thinking. Perhaps it's time I ended your punishment."

Ruby sat upright. "Really?"

Yvonne's lips curled up at the side. "Come with me and find out."

Ruby followed Yvonne into the hall, and toward Ruby's bedroom. But Yvonne strolled straight past it, continuing until they reached the bedroom next to Yvonne's.

Yvonne's 'playroom.'

Nervous excitement bubbled up inside Ruby. She hadn't returned to that room since that fateful night. She'd been waiting for Yvonne to take her back inside, to finally give her a taste of all the toys hidden in the drawers and closet.

Yvonne opened the door and pulled Ruby toward the bed. She drew Ruby into her, running her hand up the side of Ruby's thigh, over the silk of her nightie. Ruby's heart began to race. Yvonne was being unusually gentle. Considering Yvonne spent over a week tormenting Ruby, she couldn't help but be suspicious.

Yvonne grabbed the hem of Ruby's nightie. "This needs to come off." She pulled it over Ruby's head, leaving her in just her panties, then gestured toward the bed. "Why don't you get comfortable?"

As Ruby got onto the bed and lay on her side, Yvonne slipped out of her dress, revealing a matching black bra and panties made of delicate mesh trimmed with lace. Ruby stared, transfixed. Had Yvonne planned this, or did she simply walk around every single day wearing sexy lingerie underneath her fitted black dresses?

Yvonne climbed onto the bed and pushed Ruby back down to it, straddling her. Ruby drew in a hard breath.

"Have you missed this?" Yvonne drew a hand down Ruby's chest, tracing her fingers idly over her breasts. "Have you missed me?"

"Yes," Ruby murmured. "So much."

Yvonne dipped low, her lips brushing Ruby's ear. "As much as I've enjoyed watching you squirm all week, I've missed having a toy to play with."

Yvonne kissed Ruby behind her ear, using her lips to draw a line of kisses down the side of Ruby's throat, all the way to Ruby's chest. Ruby trembled. After so long without Yvonne's touch, every inch of Ruby's skin was hypersensitive, every nerve in her body primed.

Yvonne teased Ruby's nipple with her lips, coaxing a moan from deep in Ruby's chest. Her hand wandered down between Ruby's legs. Ruby's thighs quivered involuntarily.

"How long has it been since you last came?" Yvonne asked.

"I can't remember." Ruby was suddenly finding it difficult to think. Her mind was a fog of arousal.

"I hope you haven't been playing with yourself. Not without your Mistress."

Ruby shook her head. Although Yvonne hadn't explicitly forbidden it, Ruby was all too aware that her pleasure belonged to Yvonne alone.

"Good." Yvonne ran her fingertips down Ruby's slit, pressing the silk of her panties into her. "You must be dying for release by now."

"God, yes." Ruby was getting wetter by the second.

"That's too bad." Yvonne pulled back slowly. "Because I'm not going to give it to you."

What? Ruby groaned. She should have known Yvonne wasn't done toying with her.

"Oh, Ruby." Yvonne shook her head. "Did you really think I was going to let you get away with this? Didn't I tell you if you kept trying to seduce me, there would be consequences?"

Ruby bit the inside of her cheek, trying to distract herself from the fire raging within her. This was agonizing.

"Perhaps I should leave you here, as you are. A few more days should be long enough for you to learn your lesson."

Ruby bit back a curse, her head tipping back. "I can't take any more of this. I'm sorry! I won't do it again."

Yvonne considered Ruby's words for a moment. "I'm a fair Mistress. Perhaps I should give you a chance to demonstrate just how contrite you are."

"Yes," Ruby begged. "Anything."

"Anything?" Yvonne folded her arms over her chest. "You really mean that, don't you?"

Ruby nodded. "Yes, Mistress."

"I appreciate your dedication, but for now, the task I'm giving you is a simple one. Make me come. If you can manage that, then perhaps I'll consider letting you come."

Ruby flushed all over. "Yes, Mistress." She'd been waiting for this chance since that night Yvonne had fucked her in her bedroom.

"One last thing."

Yvonne leaned over and opened the top drawer of the nightstand. The drawer's contents made a metallic clink as she rustled around inside it. What was she looking for?

Ruby's mind raced with all the possibilities, each more intriguing than the last.

Finally, Yvonne produced a small velvet pouch from the drawer. She reached inside it, pulling out a long, thin silver chain. At the ends of the chain were two small silver clips. Each clip had a string of red rubies with small diamonds in between dangling from it. Each clip had a large ruby dangling from it like a teardrop.

Yvonne dangled the chain from her finger. "I had them made just for you. I thought it was time I bought my wife some jewelry."

Were those nipple clamps? Ruby stared at them, her lips parting slightly. Yvonne's twisted sense of humor aside, Ruby had to admit that they were beautiful. The silver chain was fine and delicate, and Ruby had no doubt that the gemstones were real.

Yvonne brushed Ruby's hair behind her shoulders, out of the way of her breasts. "I'll put them on."

Yvonne took Ruby's pebbled nipple in her fingertips, attaching a clamp to it. She turned a knob on the side so that the clamp squeezed tighter, making Ruby's nipple tingle and burn. Ruby sucked in a breath. The clamps were deceptive in their delicateness, the weight of the jewels hanging from them tugging at her nipple. By the time Yvonne finished attaching the other clamp, that tingling she felt had traveled all the way down to where Ruby's thighs met.

Yvonne drew back, admiring her handiwork. "Don't you look delectable?"

She gave the chain hanging from Ruby's chest a gentle

pull. Ruby gasped, a shock wave of pleasure going through her.

"Now, where were we?" Yvonne took a few stray pillows and arranged them at her back, reclining against them. She slid her hands down to her waist and peeled her panties down her legs before parting her thighs. "Go on. Prove to me that you deserve to be released from your punishment."

Without hesitation, Ruby crawled between Yvonne's legs, gliding a hand up the inside of Yvonne's thigh. She wanted to savor the moment, to take things slow and explore every inch of the other woman's body, but she was dying to come herself. Yvonne had kept her on edge for so long, and Ruby ached for her. Only she could give Ruby what she needed.

But first, Ruby had to give her Mistress what she needed.

Ruby buried herself between Yvonne's thighs, her head filling with the other woman's sweet scent, her lips grazing the soft hair that covered Yvonne's nether lips. Ruby slipped her tongue between them, relishing the woman's silky heat.

A murmur rose from Yvonne's chest. "Yes. Show me how much you've missed your Mistress's touch."

Ruby drew her tongue up to Yvonne's clit and painted soft spirals around it. A deep sigh fell from Yvonne's lips, invigorating Ruby. She grabbed onto the sides of Yvonne's hips to anchor herself. The motion caused the heavy jewels dangling from the nipple clamps to swing, sending a bolt of pleasure through her. The moan Ruby let out was muffled by her Mistress's thighs.

It only seemed to turn Yvonne on even more. She grabbed onto the back of Ruby's head with both hands, guiding Ruby as she swept and rolled her tongue, sucking, licking, and teasing.

"Oh, yes," Yvonne said. "Oh, yes…"

Yvonne ground back against Ruby, her moans building and building. Finally, she rose up into Ruby, a strangled cry erupting from her mouth. Her thighs clenched and her body thrashed, her orgasm consuming her.

Yvonne's hands slipped from Ruby's head. Ruby eased away, kneeling on the bed between her Mistress's legs, awaiting her command. Had Ruby earned her release? She'd certainly given Yvonne hers.

After a moment's rest, Yvonne sat up and gave the chain of the nipple clamps a playful tug. Ruby let out a quivering breath, to Yvonne's clear amusement.

"I can say with confidence that you've proven yourself," she said. "Your punishment is over. You've earned a reward."

Ruby sighed with relief. *Finally!* But when Yvonne reached into the nightstand again, Ruby's stomach flipped. Was Yvonne still not finished toying with her?

This time, Yvonne only pulled out a pair of leather cuffs. "You know what to do."

Ruby held out her wrists obediently. At this point, Ruby would do anything her Mistress wanted, as long as Yvonne gave her release.

Yvonne fastened the cuffs around Ruby's wrists, the smooth leather caressing her skin. Yvonne drew Ruby's arms up above her head, took the short chain hanging from one of the cuffs, and threaded it around a bar on the headboard. She clipped the free end to the other cuff, leaving Ruby bound to the bed by her wrists. Ruby's heart began to pound.

Yvonne ran a hand down Ruby's arm. "Close your eyes. Your Mistress will take care of everything."

Ruby took in a deep breath and shut her eyes. She felt Yvonne's hands at her sides, her fingers slipping beneath the waistband of Ruby's panties, peeling them from Ruby's legs. Ruby throbbed with anticipation.

Yvonne nudged Ruby's knees apart and slid her hand into Ruby's slit. Ruby shuddered, her eyes rolling into her head. She'd been waiting so long for her Mistress's touch that the slightest brush of Yvonne's fingers sent electricity sparking through her.

Yvonne traced a finger up to circle Ruby's bud. Ruby let out an uncontrollable moan.

"Don't even think about coming yet," Yvonne said. "I'm still having my fun with you."

With her free hand, Yvonne reached up and tugged on the nipple clamps. Ruby hissed. She'd forgotten she was wearing them. She certainly remembered now. Her nipples tingled and burned, only bringing her closer to a climax.

Yvonne ran her hand down to Ruby's entrance and dipped a finger inside, then another. A shiver of pleasure went through Ruby. She pushed back against Yvonne's fingers, desperate to fill the hollowness within her.

"Had enough?" Yvonne drew her fingers in and out with an unbearable slowness. "Want me to give you what you need?"

"Yes," Ruby whimpered. "*Please.*"

"All right, pet. You've earned it."

Yvonne pumped her fingers harder and deeper, the heel of her palm grinding against Ruby's aching clit. Ruby convulsed against Yvonne, delirious, her fingers curling and her wrists straining against the cuffs.

"Go on," Yvonne said. "You can come now."

At once, the pleasure inside Ruby rose and rose. Just as it reached a crescendo, Yvonne reached up and slipped her fingers under the chain of the nipple clamps, pulling them from Ruby's nipples.

"Oh!" The rush of blood and sensation sent Ruby over the edge. She arched into Yvonne as an earth-shattering orgasm consumed her entire body. Yvonne surged inside her, sending Ruby deeper and deeper into sweet oblivion, until she was certain she was going to be swept away.

As Ruby returned to reality, breathless and weak, Yvonne began uncuffing Ruby's hands. She sank into the bed, the feeling of her Mistress's fingers on the insides of her wrists making her skin tingle. Yvonne freed Ruby from her restraints and kissed her slowly. Ruby pressed herself against her Mistress, devouring her Mistress's lips.

Yvonne wrapped her arms around Ruby, drawing her down to the bed. "Come here."

Ruby snuggled in closer, grateful that she didn't need to ask Yvonne to hold her. She wasn't the type to feel needy after sex, but right now, Ruby wanted nothing more than to spend the rest of the night in Yvonne's arms. This insatiable need for closeness only ever came about when she played these kinds of intimate, kinky games with Yvonne.

Ruby's stomach stirred. Was she developing feelings for Yvonne, or was she simply feeling the way she was because of the complicated nature of their relationship? Yvonne was so many things to her. 'Wife.' Mistress. Partner in crime in an elaborate inheritance scheme. Ruby was irrevocably bound to her, and all the ties between them were beginning to tangle.

Regardless of what she felt toward Yvonne, one thing was certain. Ruby was in too deep now, under Yvonne's spell, addicted to their kinky games.

And last time that had happened, she'd almost ended up broken.

CHAPTER 15

Yvonne woke the next morning, weighed down by an awful, sinking feeling. It was like her entire body was made of wet sand.

She rolled over in the playroom bed. She and Ruby had fallen asleep in it the night before. But now, Ruby was nowhere to be seen.

Yvonne dragged herself out of bed, a feat that took far more effort than it should have, and headed for the kitchen. Her head felt foggy. She needed coffee.

As she entered the kitchen, she was almost knocked over by Ruby.

"Oops, sorry!" Ruby clutched the cup of coffee she'd almost spilled on Yvonne. "I'm running late."

"You have plans?" Yvonne asked. It was the weekend.

Ruby nodded. "I've been exploring the city a lot more lately, and I found this amazing day spa uptown, so I thought I'd treat myself." A guilty look crossed her face. "It's a bit pricey. Actually, it's really, really pricey. I hope you don't mind."

"It's fine, Ruby. You don't need to ask my permission to spend money."

"Right. Guess it's a habit. Anyway, it'll definitely be worth it. I booked in a whole day of pampering and indulgence. I invited someone along too. My cousin, Brooke. I found out she lives here now, so I reached out to her."

"Good for you," Yvonne said.

"Don't worry, I won't tell her the truth about our arrangement. I'll keep up the charade with her too." Ruby looked at Yvonne's face, frowning. "Is everything okay?"

"I'm still waking up, that's all," Yvonne lied. "Some coffee will help."

"All right. I need to get going, but I'll be back this afternoon."

"I'll be out most of the day too. Maid of honor business with Madison."

"Sounds like fun. I'll see you later." Ruby smiled at Yvonne before leaving the room.

As soon as Ruby was gone, that sense of dread came over Yvonne again. What was wrong with her? Was she sick? She felt like she'd been sucked into a black hole. She wanted nothing more than to crawl back into bed, but she'd promised Madison she'd help her with some last-minute wedding planning.

A cup of coffee, a shower, and a short cab ride later, Yvonne knocked on the door to Madison's apartment. After a few seconds, a bubbly redheaded woman answered the door. Blair, Madison's fiancée.

"Yvonne, hi." Blair smiled. "Come on in."

Yvonne greeted her and followed her inside.

"I'm about to head out, but Madison is around here

somewhere." Blair led Yvonne into the lounge room. "Have a seat. By the way, it was fun meeting Ruby at Lilith's the other night. Are you bringing her to the wedding?"

Yvonne sat down. "I don't know yet."

"She's welcome to come. We can make room for her. You know, the two of you should come over for dinner sometime."

Yvonne made a noise of assent as Blair continued. Yvonne wasn't in the mood to chat. Although she liked Blair, the woman's bubbly enthusiasm was too much for Yvonne right now. She simply couldn't shake the dark mood she was in.

A minute later, Madison entered the room, a cup of coffee in her hand. "Yvonne, you're here."

"I'll leave you two to it," Blair said. "Have fun." She planted a kiss on Madison's cheek before bouncing toward the door.

Madison took a seat next to Yvonne. "Thank you for agreeing to help out. There's still so much to do. Who knew weddings were so much work?"

"It's no problem," Yvonne murmured.

Madison set her coffee down, frowning. "Is something the matter?"

Yvonne shook her head. "Everything's fine."

"Yvonne, you know you can't lie to me. What's wrong?"

"I don't know, okay?" Yvonne closed her eyes for a moment, drawing in a breath. "I don't know what's wrong with me. I just woke up feeling… off."

"Off how?"

"It's hard to explain. It's like I spent the whole night

drinking and now I have a dreadful hangover. Except, I didn't drink a thing last night."

"What *did* you do last night?"

Yvonne paused. "Remember when I told you Ruby and I weren't having sex?"

Madison raised an eyebrow. "Yes?"

"Well, let's just say we're doing far more than that. And it was Ruby who initiated it, not me."

"Ah. I suspected as much. So when you brought Ruby to Lilith's Den, that wasn't just for show?"

"No, it wasn't."

Madison leaned back and crossed her arms. "I think I know what's happening here. Let me guess. Last night the two of you did a scene?"

Yvonne nodded.

"And this morning you woke up feeling like crap?"

"Yes. Where are you going with this, Madison?"

Madison tilted her head, scrutinizing Yvonne. "This really hasn't happened to you before?"

"No. And what's 'this?'"

"You're familiar with the concept of subdrop?"

"Of course." Yvonne had explained it to Ruby that night after Lilith's Den.

"This is the same thing. It's like a kind of hangover that sometimes comes after a scene." Madison crossed her legs. "Let me guess. On top of feeling exhausted, you feel depressed. Guilty. Concerned about hurting Ruby?"

Yvonne nodded. She hadn't been able to put her feelings into words, but what Madison was describing was exactly how she felt.

"It's common, and completely normal. As a Domme, you

engage in activities that most people consider twisted and perverse, things that are potentially harmful and dangerous. Your subconscious can have a hard time processing all that. Combine that with the physical and mental strain of constantly maintaining control? If you're not careful, it can lead to a crash. It happens to the best of us."

That couldn't possibly be what Yvonne was experiencing. After all, what she and Ruby had done the night before wasn't anything extreme, especially not by Yvonne's standards. She was still taking it slow with Ruby, working out where Ruby's limits were. But there was no other explanation for what Yvonne was feeling.

"So you've experienced this?" she asked.

"In the past," Madison replied. "Now I know the signs so I can stave it off before it sets in. It's easy enough. You deal with it the same way you deal with your submissive dropping. Aftercare. But instead of you only focusing on your sub's needs, she focuses on yours as well. Dommes need love too, you know. We make ourselves as vulnerable to our submissives as they do to us, just in a different way. We give them a side of ourselves that few people get to see."

That was a perspective Yvonne had never considered. "What do *you* do when this happens?"

"I let Blair take care of me." Madison lowered her voice, as if to prevent Blair overhearing her somehow. "Of course, she doesn't know that's what she's doing. She's simply serving her Mistress. I'll have her give me a massage, draw me a bath, bring me something to drink. It's a good excuse to have your submissive wait on you hand and foot." Madison took a sip of her coffee. "There's nothing as satisfying as getting a massage from a grateful submissive after spending the entire evening spanking her."

Yvonne held up her hand. "I get the picture. That isn't a bad idea."

"You see? I know you like to deal with your problems by yourself, but you're only human. You need to make sure your needs are met in any relationship."

"What Ruby and I have hardly counts as a relationship."

"She's your submissive, isn't she?" Madison asked.

"Yes, but that's all. I'm paying her to play my wife. I have no feelings toward her."

"No feelings? Yvonne, you're not that heartless."

"Fine, I care about her. Of course I do. But not in the way you're suggesting."

Madison studied Yvonne's face. "Did it ever occur to you that you're experiencing this drop for the first time because this is the first time you've had a submissive you actually care about? Having that genuine connection really heightens everything. It makes all those feelings and emotions that come with BDSM play even more intense."

Was there some truth to what Madison was saying? Normally, Yvonne kept herself emotionally detached when it came to these kinds of relationships. They were physical and psychological, nothing more. But she couldn't deny the connection she felt with Ruby. With Ruby, Yvonne found it easier than ever to let go, to lose herself in the sensual experience they were sharing.

However, that didn't mean there was anything romantic there. "I'm sorry to disappoint you, but I don't have those kinds of feelings toward Ruby," Yvonne said. "I care about her as my submissive. That's *all*."

"If you say so," Madison murmured.

Yvonne narrowed her eyes. "You were never this smug until you and Blair got engaged."

"What can I say?" Madison's expression grew wistful. "Love changes a woman."

Yvonne resisted the urge to roll her eyes. Since Madison and Blair had gotten together, Madison had gone from being just as disinterested in relationships as Yvonne to being completely lovesick. Although Yvonne was happy that Madison had found love, one of the irritating side effects of Madison's transformation was that she kept trying to fix everyone else's love lives. Yvonne's love life didn't need fixing. She didn't have one to begin with. She wasn't interested in relationships. She was perfectly happy being alone. She'd been alone her entire life, so she was used to it. It was easier that way.

But wasn't she happier now that Ruby was in her life?

"While we're on the subject, is Ruby coming to the wedding?" Madison asked.

"I haven't asked her yet," Yvonne said. Would Ruby be able to handle such a task? Playing happily married couple for a handful of Yvonne's friends at a club was one thing, but the wedding of Madison Sloane, the billionaire founder of Mistress Media, was a huge event. There would be hundreds of people there. "I'll talk to her and get back to you. Now, let's get started with this wedding business. What do you need my help with?"

CHAPTER 16

"God," Brooke said. "I'm so relaxed I could drown."

Ruby murmured in agreement, breathing in all the scents wafting up from the spa they were sitting in. She wasn't quite sure what was in the water, but it included tea, flowers, and all kinds of heavenly things. Between the spa she was soaking in and the earlier massage and body scrub, Ruby was feeling more relaxed than she thought possible.

Brooke turned to her. "Thanks again for inviting me. We're long overdue for a catch up. Plus, this place is incredible. I could never afford to come here myself."

"It's no problem," Ruby replied. "I wanted to see you."

"How can you even afford somewhere as fancy as this?" Brooke asked. "No offense, but the last I heard, you were waitressing in Vegas. That was years ago. You kind of dropped off the radar there."

Ruby felt a pang of guilt. "I know. I'm sorry about that." She and Brooke had been close as kids. With four brothers, Ruby had appreciated having another girl around growing up. But Ruby had lost touch with her cousin in recent years.

She'd lost touch with everyone, from her family to her friends. Her last client, who she refused to think of as an ex, had isolated her from them, slowly, without her noticing until it was too late.

But that was all behind her now. It was time Ruby started rebuilding her life.

"For what it's worth, I've really missed you," she said.

"It's okay," Brooke said. "I get it. Life happens. And I've missed you too." She smiled. "So, what's the deal? You're obviously doing well for yourself these days."

"I'm not waitressing anymore. I got married, actually." Ruby hadn't had a chance to tell Brooke about Yvonne yet. They'd been too busy getting pampered.

"Seriously? When?"

"It's kind of a recent thing."

"Wow," Brooke said. "Congrats. Who's the lucky gal or guy?"

"Her name's Yvonne. We met while I was… waitressing."

"Ooh, don't tell me. She's totally loaded?" Brooke wasn't exactly tactful.

Ruby shrugged. "Something like that."

"Wow. So you bagged yourself a rich wife. I want to hear all about it. Start from the beginning."

Ruby took a deep breath and began telling Brooke the fake story of how she and Yvonne had met. This time, she found herself embellishing the details, spinning a tale far more romantic than the reality. It came easily to her. Lately, Ruby had found herself fantasizing about her relationship with Yvonne, wondering what it would be like if everything between them was real. What if Yvonne had picked Ruby up at work one night, swept her off her feet, fallen madly in love with her? What if the two of them had truly gotten married and moved in together, living the perfect, happy life that they pretended to share?

Of course, Yvonne's idea of a perfect marriage probably involved handcuffs and collars, but Ruby was starting to feel like that was her idea of a perfect relationship too. What was more romantic than surrendering oneself to someone as deeply as Ruby was to Yvonne? What was more intimate than trusting someone so completely?

"Wow," Brooke said, once Ruby was finished. "That's like something from a movie. Your family must be so happy. I'm surprised your mom hasn't mentioned it."

Ruby murmured a vague excuse. She hadn't actually told her mother about her marriage yet. Ruby hadn't spoken to her, or her father and brothers, since she'd left Vegas. She rarely spoke about relationships with her family, mostly because of her job. Even when she'd been with her former client, she hadn't told them about him. She'd hidden him from them, so they wouldn't know the truth about how he treated her.

Ruby made a mental note to call her family. She missed them, and she hoped they'd forgive her for falling out of touch. What would happen when she told her family about Yvonne? Would they all want to speak with Ruby's 'wife?' Ruby was certain her brothers would try to intimidate Yvonne, threatening her with all kinds of outrageous things if she dared to hurt Ruby. They were grossly overprotective, which Ruby had always found sexist and patronizing.

She smiled to herself. Perhaps letting her brothers talk to Yvonne would be a good thing. Yvonne wouldn't be intimidated by their posturing. She would put them in their place in no time at all.

Ruby shook herself. She was doing it again, thinking about her marriage to Yvonne as if it were real. She couldn't deny the appeal of this fantasy they'd created together. Perhaps it was simply the extravagant lifestyle she was living with Yvonne that appealed to her.

Although, she found Yvonne herself appealing in every way. The way she walked and moved. The luscious timbre her voice would take on when she issued Ruby a command. The way her eyes would shimmer as she tormented Ruby with all kinds of pleasures.

But that intense draw Ruby felt toward her was purely physical and mental. It was the thrill of surrendering to her Mistress that Ruby was addicted to. The alternative was that she was falling for Yvonne, and that was out of the question. Ruby couldn't fall for a client. Not again.

Brooke stretched out her arms, yawning. Ruby hadn't even noticed she'd stopped talking.

"So," Brooke said. "So, now that you've got a rich wife and you're not waitressing anymore, what are you doing with yourself?"

Ruby shrugged. "Not much, really. I'm still settling into my new life. I haven't figured out what I want to do with it yet."

That much was true. Even after the year was over, she'd have five million dollars. If she was smart, she wouldn't have to worry about money ever again. She could do anything she wanted.

But she was no closer to figuring out what it was that she wanted.

"I'd kill to have some time to do my own thing," Brooke said. "I'm working two jobs right now, and I'm thinking of picking up a third." She sighed. "Does Yvonne have any rich friends you can set me up with?"

"She does, but they're all women," Ruby replied.

"That's too bad." Brooke closed her eyes. "You have no idea how lucky you are."

Brooke had a good point. Ruby *was* lucky. She had everything she could ever need, along with the freedom to do whatever she wanted, yet she was wasting all her time lounging around the apartment, feeling lost and hopeless. She was free of her old life. She had to take advantage of that. She had to start living again.

What did that involve for her? What kind of life did Ruby want to build? What did she want to do with herself? Lately, she'd been spending half her time baking. She'd been making the most of all the supplies she'd bought, attempting more and more extravagant creations. Her skills were improving. Perhaps she had a knack for it after all.

Could she take a few classes, learn from a professional? She could even go to culinary school. She had the time, and the money. And once she was done with that? She could even open her own bakery like she'd dreamed about as a girl. It was a silly idea. Then again, Ruby would be a millionaire soon. What else was she going to do with all her money?

Her future held so many possibilities. For the first time, Ruby had total control over it. Why was the idea so overwhelming?

Ruby closed her eyes and sank deeper into the spa. She

could worry about the future later. For now, she wanted to enjoy the present.

~

When Yvonne returned home that night, she was hit by the most delicious scent. Vanilla, mingled with coffee. Ruby had to be baking again. She'd been spending lots of time in the kitchen lately.

As Yvonne passed through the apartment, she found Ruby curled up in an armchair in the living room, her nose buried in her phone. After a few seconds, Ruby noticed Yvonne and smiled.

"You're home," she said. "I have a surprise for you. It's in the kitchen. Come on."

Before Yvonne could react, Ruby got up and headed for the kitchen. Yvonne followed her, the delicious scent stronger. They reached the kitchen. Sitting on the island in the middle was an elaborately decorated cake.

"I wasn't sure what you like, so I had to make a guess," Ruby said. "I know you like coffee, and everyone likes cheesecake, so I made a coffee-flavored one. I used real coffee beans and everything."

Yvonne stared at her. "You baked me a cake?" She'd never had a lover do anything like this before. Yvonne's habit of ditching her lovers before they could get too comfortable probably had something to do with it.

"I wanted to do something nice for you. To show my appreciation. And, well-" Ruby hesitated. "I thought you could use some cheering up. You didn't seem like yourself this morning, but I didn't want to pry."

Had Yvonne been that much of a wreck in the morning, or was Ruby simply getting better at reading her? They'd been living together for almost two months now. It was no surprise that she'd picked up on some of Yvonne's quirks.

"So, is everything okay?" Ruby asked.

"Yes," Yvonne said. "Everything is fine."

"All right. How about you go sit down in the living room? I'll bring you a slice. Just put your feet up and relax, Mistress."

Yvonne went into the living room and took a seat. She could get used to having Ruby wait on her. She could already feel the cloud that had been hanging over her all day receding. Perhaps Madison had been onto something.

And Yvonne hadn't even had to ask Ruby for anything. Ruby had simply taken it upon herself to look after her Mistress's needs.

Ruby entered the room and handed Yvonne a slice of cake, before sitting down next to her, watching intently as Yvonne took a bite.

"Well?" Ruby said. "How is it?"

Yvonne put the plate and fork down on the table before her. "This is the most delicious thing I've ever tasted." She was exaggerating, but not much. Ruby's baking skills had improved.

"I'm glad you like it." Ruby kissed Yvonne on the cheek.

Yvonne felt a surge of warmth. Clearly her emotions were still all over the place. Or had Madison been right about something else too? Was Yvonne developing feelings for Ruby?

Yvonne pushed the thought aside. "Madison's wedding is coming up. How would you like to be my plus one? I should warn you, it's a big event. There will be hundreds of people there. It's a lot of pressure. Think you can handle it?"

"Sure," Ruby said. "I like a good party. And I like playing wife."

"Then you're going to need something to wear. I'll have my stylist come by during the week. I already have something in mind." Yvonne looked Ruby up and down. "You're going to look irresistible."

Ruby smiled shyly. *God, that smile.* It was the perfect antidote for Yvonne's dark mood.

Yvonne stretched out, draping an arm loosely over Ruby's shoulder. "Why don't you tell me about your day? How was catching up with your cousin?"

"It was great," Ruby said. "She was really impressed by the fact that I bagged myself a hot, rich wife."

Ruby nestled against Yvonne's shoulder and began filling her in on her day. Yvonne nodded along. Perhaps she felt more toward Ruby than she'd let herself admit, but that didn't mean those feelings were serious.

Was there any harm in indulging those feelings? It would make it far easier to keep up the pretense that they were a happily married couple. And Yvonne hadn't forgotten that it was all just an arrangement. One with an expiration date.

It could never become anything more.

CHAPTER 17

"Ruby?" Yvonne called from the master bedroom. "I need you."

"One second." Ruby had just gotten out of the shower. She hadn't even heard Yvonne come home.

She wrapped a towel around herself and headed to Yvonne's bedroom. It was the day of Madison's wedding, and Yvonne had left early in the morning to deal with maid of honor business, with the plan to return home to get dressed before the wedding itself began in the afternoon. Ruby wasn't going until later when the ceremony started.

Ruby reached Yvonne's room. Inside, Yvonne was standing in front of a full-length mirror. Her hair was gathered up in an elaborate bun, adorned with sparkling hairpins, and the sunlight streaming through the window made her eyes shift to a mesmerizing shade of green. She wore a strapless gown in an enchanting midnight blue, with a long skirt that flowed down to the floor.

Ruby's lips parted slightly. The dress was unlike anything Yvonne normally wore. She favored sleek, fitted clothing, usually in black. The blue bridesmaid's dress was almost princess-like.

But it made Yvonne look like a queen.

Yvonne spied Ruby in the mirror and pointed toward the zipper at her back. "I need your help with this."

Ruby blinked. "Sure."

Ruby walked over to her. Yvonne's bare back was smooth and toned. Ruby yearned to draw her hand up it, to wrap her arms around Yvonne and pull her close, to kiss her way down her Mistress's naked shoulders…

Pulling herself together, Ruby took the zipper and drew it up Yvonne's back, fastening the dress closed.

"Thank you." Yvonne smoothed the dress down, then squared her shoulders, standing regally before the mirror as she inspected herself. Her eyes met Ruby's through the mirror. "How do I look?"

"You're going to upstage the brides," Ruby said.

"All eyes will be on them, I'm sure."

"Not mine. I know who I'll be looking at."

The tiniest smile crossed Yvonne's lips. "I'm looking forward to seeing you in your dress too." She turned to face Ruby. "I need to head back for now. I might not see you until the reception. I'll have my hands full with maid of honor duties."

Ruby nodded. "I'll see you there."

Yvonne grabbed her purse from the nearby chair, put a hand on Ruby's waist, and gave her a soft, brief kiss on the lips before leaving the room.

As Yvonne's footsteps receded, Ruby brought her hand up to her mouth, where the echo of Yvonne's kiss remained.

Had Yvonne just kissed her goodbye?

Yvonne stood by as Madison and Blair said their vows before the watching crowd. The hours leading up to the ceremony had been punctuated by one disaster after another. Naturally, Yvonne had handled them all while making sure both the brides didn't realize anything was amiss. It hadn't been easy. Now that the ceremony was in motion, Yvonne finally had a chance to breathe.

Her eyes wandered over the sea of faces before them. It was impossible to spot Ruby in the large crowd. Yvonne couldn't stop thinking about that casual kiss she'd given Ruby earlier. It had been a reflex, something she'd done without conscious thought.

Clearly, pretending that she and Ruby were a married couple was getting to her.

Yvonne focused her attention on Madison and Blair. They slipped the rings on each other's fingers. The celebrant pronounced them married. They shared a tender kiss.

Yvonne couldn't help but feel moved by it all. She wasn't usually the sentimental type, but for a fleeting moment, she imagined herself at the altar, standing before her bride. Had she caught wedding fever from helping Madison plan her wedding? She had no interest in getting married, at least not for real.

An hour and what felt like thousands of photos later, Yvonne headed to the reception with the rest of the bridal party. After dealing with some minor issues, she got stuck in conversation with various acquaintances before finally making an excuse to slip away. Then she began searching the ballroom for Ruby.

There.

Standing by the bar was a woman even more stunning than the one Yvonne had met at the bar in Vegas. Her long blonde hair flowed over her bare shoulders and her neck was adorned in a diamond and ruby necklace. She was dressed in a floor-length gown in a deep, rich crimson with a low-cut back. It was the perfect balance of elegant and sexy.

Yvonne had chosen the dress, but she hadn't dreamed Ruby would look so incredible in it.

Ruby spotted Yvonne and headed over to her.

"Ruby." Yvonne looked her up and down once more. "You look wonderful."

"What can I say? You have great taste." Ruby gave her a coy smile. "You know, I was wearing a red dress the night we met."

"How could I forget? You looked so tantalizing that night." Yvonne didn't miss the flush that crossed Ruby's cheeks at her words. "Let's go mingle. We need to keep up appearances."

"Come on, Yvonne." Ruby stepped in close and gave Yvonne a sultry look, speaking under her breath. "We both know this isn't about appearances."

Yvonne frowned. "What do you mean?"

"I think you were lying when you said you don't care about showing me off," Ruby teased. "I think you like walking around with a pretty woman on your arm."

Yvonne let out a small chuckle. "You're right. There's certainly something satisfying about being here with the prettiest woman in the room." She held her arm out to Ruby. "Come on. Let's go show you off."

Ruby took Yvonne's arm. They grabbed some champagne and made their way through the hall. By now, the party was in full swing, the packed ballroom bustling with activity. Yvonne introduced Ruby to various friends and acquaintances. Most of them couldn't hide their surprise at Yvonne's newlywed status and began probing them both for details.

Yvonne shouldn't have worried that the wedding would be too much for Ruby. Ruby handled it all with poise. She was utterly convincing as Yvonne's wife.

After a conversation with a particularly nosy college friend of Yvonne's, she and Ruby wandered off to find Madison. It had been some time since Yvonne had checked in with her, and as maid of honor, she felt obliged to keep an eye on everything.

They found Madison nearby, talking with Lydia, the only one of Yvonne's friends who hadn't met Ruby yet. Although Yvonne and Lydia weren't close, Yvonne had a certain respect for the woman. They were similar in a lot of ways.

"Lydia, this is my wife, Ruby," Yvonne said. "Ruby, Lydia. Lydia joined Mistress recently as our CFO. And you've already met Madison."

Ruby greeted them both.

"Nice to meet you," Lydia said. "I was just telling Madison how lovely the ceremony was."

"It was, wasn't it?" Ruby let out a wistful sigh. "This is all so romantic. It makes me wish Yvonne and I had had a real ceremony."

Yvonne gave her a sharp glance. What was Ruby doing? Perhaps she'd had a few too many glasses of champagne.

"That's right," Lydia said. "Your wedding was a spontaneous affair, wasn't it?"

"That's one way of putting it," Ruby replied. "There were no bridesmaids, no reception, just a priest dressed as Elvis and two cheap gold-plated wedding bands." She slipped her hand into Yvonne's. "But it was romantic in its own way, don't you think so, honey?"

Honey? It was clear that Ruby was enjoying playing wife far too much. But two could play at that game.

Yvonne gave Ruby her best longing gaze. "It was. But perhaps one day we can have a do-over. A real wedding."

Ruby beamed. "Really?"

"Why not? Whatever you want, it's yours. How about on our anniversary? A year, or two, from now, perhaps?"

Ruby leaned over and planted a kiss on Yvonne's cheek. "I'd love that."

As the conversation moved on, Yvonne noticed Madison staring at them both, a slight frown on her face. Yvonne had thought Madison had gotten over her disapproval of Yvonne and Ruby's arrangement. She let go of Ruby's hand. Perhaps it was a sign they were laying it on too thick.

But Ruby didn't notice. She was happily recounting the story of how they'd 'met' to Lydia. Somehow, it had gotten even longer and more elaborate than before.

When the conversation finally lulled, Madison glanced toward the other side of the room, then grimaced. "Christ, my uncle is showing Blair photos on his phone again. I need to go rescue her."

"I'll take care of it," Yvonne said.

"Yvonne, you've been putting out fires all evening. I can handle this. Just relax and enjoy the party." Before Yvonne could protest, Madison turned to Ruby. "Thank you for coming, Ruby. Enjoy the rest of the night. And make sure your wife here has some fun, will you?"

Ruby grinned. "I'll try my best."

Madison shot Yvonne a knowing look before walking away.

Lydia took the cue to head to the bar, leaving Yvonne and Ruby alone. Yvonne turned to her 'wife.'

"So," she said. "You wish we had a real wedding, do you?"

Ruby gave an innocent shrug. "If I'm going to get married, I want to do it properly. What happened in Vegas wasn't exactly my idea of a dream wedding."

Yvonne raised an eyebrow. "So you were one of those girls with the scrapbook full of cutouts from wedding magazines?"

"Not really. I was never much of a romantic, and when I went into my line of work, I threw the idea of getting married any time soon out the window. But I don't plan to be an escort forever. And I hope that one day I'll find that special someone, and we'll get to share a special day."

"Tell me. What would that special day look like?"

Ruby thought for a moment. "It would be small, for starters. Nothing like this. Just family and friends. Maybe in the countryside, or on the beach. Somewhere quiet, where we'd be surrounded by nature and the people we love."

That actually sounded… nice. Yvonne had never been interested in weddings, but now, she was starting to understand the appeal. There was a certain magic about them.

"And I know it's cliché, but I like the idea of becoming a princess for a day." Ruby's cheeks flushed, a dreamy look in her eyes. "I want to dress up in a beautiful dress. I want to walk down the aisle. I want my bride to lift up my veil and look at me like I'm her whole world. I want us to read our vows and exchange rings, and I want her to kiss me, and it would be this magical moment where the rest of the world would fade away and it would just be you and me-"

Ruby covered her mouth with her hand, her face turning crimson. It took even longer for Yvonne to register what Ruby had said. Not *her*.

You.

"I didn't-" The blush on Ruby's face deepened. "It was a slip of the tongue."

Yvonne stared at her. "Ruby…"

Yvonne was cut off by a voice calling her name. Her blood turned to ice. It was a familiar voice, but one she hadn't expected to hear at Madison's wedding.

She turned to see a man standing nearby, tall with sandy blond hair. Like everyone else in Yvonne's family, he looked nothing like her, save for the hazel color of his eyes.

"It *is* you," Yvonne's brother said.

"Nicholas." Yvonne couldn't hide her displeasure. "What are you doing here?"

"I'm here with a date." He cocked his head toward a woman standing nearby, texting on her phone. "Jane Porter. We just started seeing each other. She needed a plus one for the wedding, so I volunteered."

The woman looked vaguely familiar. She must have been one of Madison's friends. Did Madison know the woman had brought Yvonne's brother as a date? Probably not, or Madison would have warned Yvonne.

"I had no idea this was your friend Madison's wedding," Nicholas said. "What a coincidence."

"It's a small world." Yvonne didn't know whether to believe him or not. Even if he had known Yvonne was coming to the wedding, he wouldn't have told her that he was coming. He would have jumped on an opportunity to catch Yvonne off guard.

"Well?" Nicholas looked pointedly at Ruby. "Aren't you going to introduce me to your date?"

Yvonne had been dreading this moment. "Ruby, this is my brother, Nicholas. Nicholas, this is Ruby. She's my wife."

Ruby couldn't hide her surprise that the man before her was Yvonne's brother, but she pulled herself together quickly. "Nice to meet you."

Nicholas looked Ruby up and down. "Likewise. I'd heard rumors of your marriage, Yvonne, but I couldn't believe it." He scoffed. "My sister? Married?"

Yvonne spoke through gritted teeth. "The rumors are true. Ruby and I are married, and happily so."

"You misunderstand me. I was simply surprised that my sister got married and I didn't get an invitation to the wedding."

Sure, that was what he meant. "It was a spontaneous decision. There was no real wedding." Yvonne didn't elaborate. She hadn't told Nicholas about her marriage for a good reason. He knew all about the conditions of Yvonne's inheritance. She was certain that he already considered the money his, since Yvonne had shown no signs of getting married in the past.

Now that things had changed, Nicholas wouldn't be happy.

"Well, congratulations to the both of you," Nicholas said. "I trust you're bringing Ruby to our family dinner?"

"I wasn't planning to." Yvonne had no intention of subjecting Ruby to her family's general unpleasantness, let alone a full-on interrogation.

"You must bring her," Nicholas said. "Mother will insist. Besides, she's *family* now, remember?"

Yvonne held back a curse. Her annual family dinner was more than just a dinner. It had been her father's wish for his wife and children to get together once a year, along with both his children's future children and spouses. Just to drive the point home, he'd written it into his will. Yvonne's inheritance was dependent on it. Yvonne had forgotten all about the 'spouses and children' clause.

Nicholas was right. Yvonne had no choice. "I'll talk to Ruby about it."

"She's right here, isn't she?" Nicholas addressed Ruby. "Dinner is next Friday. It's at our family home in the mountains. Are you available? We'd love to have you join us."

"Er," Ruby glanced at Yvonne. "Sure. I can come."

"Then it's settled." Nicholas looked over his shoulder toward his date. "I should get back to Jane. I'll see you both at dinner. Mother will be so delighted to hear of your marriage."

He flashed Yvonne a smile, his eyes gleaming wickedly. Yvonne's stomach dropped. Nicholas knew. He'd made the connection between Yvonne's marriage and the inheritance money. He was already scheming behind those eyes of his.

He was going to try to stop Yvonne from getting her inheritance.

Nicholas turned and walked away. As soon as he was out of earshot, Yvonne cursed.

"What's the matter?" Ruby asked her.

"Nothing." Yvonne didn't want to stress Ruby out with the news that someone was threatening their marriage scheme right now. They were in a high enough pressure situation as it was. "I just wasn't expecting to see him here."

"Your brother? He didn't seem so bad."

"Trust me, he's not the perfect gentleman he appears to be," Yvonne said. "I'm sorry for putting you on the spot like that."

"It's fine. What's this dinner, anyway?"

"Once a year, we have dinner at my family home. It's just me, Nicholas, and my stepmother, Alice. It's a bit of a trek, so we usually stay overnight. That's all there is to it, really."

Ruby frowned. "You only have dinner with your family once a year?"

"In case you couldn't tell, we're not particularly close. You'll have to trust me when I say my family dynamics are… complicated. But now isn't the time for all that. This is a wedding. We're supposed to be enjoying ourselves."

"I'm definitely enjoying myself. Dressing up, drinking champagne, meeting all these people. I'm having a great time. We should do this more often."

"Isn't this normal for you?" Yvonne asked. "You said yourself that your clients love to take you out and show you off."

"That's true. But this is different. It feels different, with you." Ruby glanced down at her feet. "What I mean is, this doesn't feel like work. I'm genuinely enjoying it. Being here, with you. Being your wife."

Yvonne felt warmth rising within her. "And I'm enjoying having you as my wife." She held out her arm to Ruby. "Let's get back to playing happy couple."

Ruby peered up at her. "Does playing happy couple involve dancing?"

Yvonne gave Ruby a stern look. "Under no circumstances."

As Ruby took her arm again, Yvonne recalled Ruby's earlier slip of the tongue. Surely it hadn't meant anything. Ruby didn't think about Yvonne that way.

Did she?

CHAPTER 18

Ruby lay in bed, staring up at the ceiling. She was glad to be home. She and Yvonne had remained at Madison and Blair's reception until the last of the guests had left. In the end, Ruby had taken to the dance floor while Yvonne had watched from the sidelines.

The entire time, Yvonne hadn't been able to take her eyes off Ruby.

But as soon as they'd returned home, they'd gone straight to their bedrooms, exhausted. And now that Ruby was in bed, she was wide awake. She still had Yvonne on her mind, along with that stupid slip-up she'd made.

Ruby sighed and got out of bed, giving up on sleep entirely. She left her bedroom, intending to head to the kitchen to grab something to drink. Instead, her feet carried her in the other direction, further down the hall and to Yvonne's bedroom door.

She paused in front of it, then knocked.

"Come in," Yvonne called from inside.

Ruby opened the door and stepped into the room. It was

lit only by the lamp on the nightstand. Yvonne stood in front of her dresser, brushing her long, dark hair out.

She glanced at Ruby. "Is there something you want?"

Ruby wasn't even sure why she'd come here. "I couldn't sleep, that's all. Thought I'd come see if you were still awake."

"I was about to get into bed." Yvonne put the hairbrush down and turned to Ruby. "Why don't you join me?"

Ruby smiled. "Sure."

Yvonne gave her a firm look. "To sleep *only*. I'm much too tired for anything else." She waved toward the bed. "Make yourself comfortable. I'll join you in a moment." She disappeared into her bathroom.

Ruby pulled back the covers on Yvonne's pristine bed and slid between the soft sheets. Somehow, it seemed cozier than her own bed. Ruby had never slept in it before. She hadn't even been inside this room since that day she went snooping.

After a few minutes, Yvonne returned, turning off the light and slipping into the bed next to Ruby, her eyes falling closed as soon as her head hit the pillow. The room was still half lit by the moonlight streaming around the blinds. It gave Yvonne's skin a pale glow.

"Yvonne?" Ruby whispered.

Yvonne stirred slightly. "Mm?"

Ruby hesitated. What did she want to say to Yvonne? What did Ruby want from her in the first place? Every time she thought she'd come close to figuring it out, she'd catch herself wanting something more from Yvonne, something inexplicable and intangible.

Yvonne rolled onto her side, propping herself up on one elbow. "What is it?"

Ruby said the first thing that came to her mind. "Why do you want your inheritance so badly? What I mean is, it doesn't seem like you need the money."

"You're right," Yvonne said. "I don't need it, but it's a lot of money. I'd be crazy to let it go."

Ruby turned to face her. "But marrying someone you don't even know for it? That's extreme. What do you plan to do with the money?"

"To start with, five million of it is going to you. As for the rest? A few million is going toward helping someone I care about. A friend of mine. She was my nanny growing up."

"You're doing this for your former nanny?"

"Nita wasn't just my nanny. She was far more, and she still is. She's family."

"So that's who Nita is."

Yvonne frowned at Ruby. "Have I mentioned her name before?"

"Just in passing," Ruby said quickly. She wasn't going to admit she'd snooped in Yvonne's study and had found the check made out to Nita in the very week she'd moved in.

"Well, she's in some financial trouble," Yvonne continued. "I want to solve her money problems once and for all. Pay off her family's debts, her house, send her kids to college. Make sure she's set for life."

"That's so generous of you." Ruby couldn't deny her surprise.

"Don't get the wrong idea, I'm not doing this just for her. I'm keeping most of my inheritance for myself. I lost some money in investments recently, so I need to rebuild my portfolio."

"Well, it's sweet of you to want to help Nita. She must be really special to you."

"She is." A small smile crossed Yvonne's lips. "Perhaps I should introduce the two of you. I think you'd like her."

"I'd love that. I am already meeting the rest of your family, after all."

Yvonne's smile faded. "About that. I'm going to think of some way to get you out of it."

"Why don't you want me to go?"

"You don't understand my family. They're toxic. And did I mention my inheritance goes to my brother if I don't claim it?"

Ruby nodded.

"I have no doubt that Nicholas and my stepmother are going to feel threatened and resentful now that I'm stealing the money out from under them. At best, they'll simply spend the whole night interrogating you, trying to expose you as a 'gold digger.' At worst, my brother will use the opportunity to try to prevent us from getting the inheritance, and he's not afraid to play dirty. If he finds a hole in our story, he'll take advantage of it."

Ruby touched Yvonne's arm reassuringly. "Then we'll have to make sure there are no holes in our story. Didn't tonight prove how good I am at playing the role of your wife?"

"It's not you I'm worried about," Yvonne muttered.

"If your family is that bad, why are you going at all?"

"It was my father's dying wish that his family get together once a year. And because he likes pulling the strings, even from beyond the grave, he wrote it into his will. My inheritance is dependent on me going. Spouses are supposed to attend too, but I'm going to get you out of this. It's simple enough just to pretend you had some kind of emergency."

"Yvonne, it's fine. I can handle it." Ruby crossed her arms. "I'm coming, and that's that."

Yvonne narrowed her eyes. "That's that?"

Ruby felt herself flush under Yvonne's intense stare. "Yes. That's that."

Before Ruby could blink, her Mistress was above her, pinning her back to the bed with nothing but her gaze.

"Someone is being awfully bossy."

Ruby's breath caught in her chest. The look in her Mistress's eyes was the very same one she'd had before she'd spanked Ruby over the kitchen bench.

"You know what?" Yvonne said. "I'm not so tired anymore."

Yvonne took Ruby's wrists and drew them above Ruby's head, holding them against the pillow with the slightest of effort. Ruby's pulse began to flutter. Was she in for some kind of kinky punishment for daring to challenge her Mistress?

Instead, Yvonne asked her a question. "When you came in here tonight, what were you looking for?"

Ruby's lips opened. *I don't know,* she tried to say. But as she looked back into Yvonne's eyes, she realized she knew exactly what it was that she wanted.

"I want you," Ruby said softly. "I just want you."

The air in the room grew cool and still. Yvonne didn't speak. She didn't move. She just continued to stare down at

Ruby, her expression unchanging. Ruby trembled underneath her, awaiting her Mistress's direction.

Wordlessly, Yvonne got up from the bed. Her eyes searched the room, landing on a nearby chair over which her bridesmaid dress was hung.

Ruby watched as Yvonne walked over to the chair. She took the dress and pulled the sash around the waist from it before returning to the bed.

Yvonne held the sash up before her, issuing a command. "Sit up and close your eyes."

Ruby obeyed. Yvonne tied the sash around Ruby's eyes, shrouding her in disorienting darkness. Her heart began to pound.

"You want me? Now you have me, and only me." Yvonne pushed Ruby back down to the bed again, speaking into her ear in a low purr. "Forget about the rest of the world. Forget about everything else. Surrender to your Mistress."

There was so much Ruby wanted to forget about. This crazy marriage plot. All the conflict and confusion she felt about Yvonne. Ruby's fears about falling for her.

Would it hurt to forget about it all, just for a moment?

"I'm all yours," Ruby said softly.

At once, Yvonne's lips crashed against hers in an unrelenting kiss, drawing the last of the breath from Ruby's lungs. She dissolved into her Mistress, the sudden burst of passion overwhelming her. Yvonne pulled at Ruby's t-shirt, drawing it over her head in one swift motion.

Ruby let out a sharp breath. She heard the swish of clothing, then Yvonne was on top of her once more, bare skin against bare skin, her breasts against Ruby's chest, hard nipples pressing into her. Ruby clutched blindly at the other woman, the thirst within her growing.

She groaned. "Yvonne..."

Yvonne trailed her lips down Ruby's neck, lower and lower, letting her teeth graze and bite into the soft parts of Ruby's shoulders and breasts. Ruby shivered, trying her hardest to calm the flame within her, but it was hopeless. Her need for Yvonne was too great.

"Please," she murmured. "I want you."

Yvonne paid her no mind, continuing her slow, painstaking descent down Ruby's body, trailing her lips over every inch of Ruby's skin. When she finally reached the base of Ruby's stomach, Ruby thought she was going to burst. The whimper that flew from her sounded wholly unfamiliar to her ears.

Yvonne took the waistband of Ruby's panties and peeled them down, drawing them from her legs. She pushed Ruby's knees apart carefully, positioning herself between them, and ran her hands along Ruby's thighs.

Goosebumps sprouted on Ruby's skin. Yvonne wrapped her arms around Ruby's upper thighs, yanking her down the bed and closer to her. Ruby gasped softly. Although she was blindfolded, she could feel the warmth of Yvonne's breath between her legs, and the brush of Yvonne's hair on the insides of her thighs.

Not a heartbeat later, Yvonne's lips were against Ruby's folds, soft and supple and warm. Yvonne slipped her tongue into Ruby's slit, searing her to her core. She sucked on Ruby's aching bud, sending jolt after jolt of pleasure through her. She grabbed onto Ruby's hips and thighs, digging into them with her fingers. Ruby's hand fell loosely to cling to the side of Yvonne's neck, needing something to hold onto in the darkness.

Finally, she couldn't take any more. Yvonne's name tumbled from her lips as ecstasy overcame her. She writhed on the bed, swept up in an ocean of pleasure, holding onto her Mistress like an anchor.

As her orgasm receded, the feeling of blissful lightness that came with it remained. When Yvonne shifted up the bed and kissed her, her own taste still on Yvonne's lips, that feeling only intensified.

Ruby sighed into the kiss, pressing herself back against Yvonne. Despite the blindfold, Ruby could see the woman before her clearly, her other senses mingling and mixing. Yvonne's fingers whispered along Ruby's skin. Her heartbeat hummed against Ruby's cheek. Her scent, perfume with a hint of sweat, was sweet and salty on Ruby's tongue.

Ruby savored it all, all those pieces of Yvonne. All the while, her hands roamed Yvonne's body, feeling every curve and dip, tracing over her pebbled nipples, sweeping over the swell of her hips. Just as Ruby was sure she had explored every part of her, Yvonne took Ruby's hand and guided it down her stomach, over the fine velvety hair at the apex of her thighs, and down between her nether lips.

Yvonne released Ruby's hand, but Ruby knew it was a signal to continue. She skated her fingertip over Yvonne's tiny, hidden clit, coaxing a soft gasp from her. She circled it gently until she felt Yvonne quiver against her.

She eased off, sliding her fingers down to the other woman's hot, throbbing entrance. Yvonne arched against Ruby's hand, urging her on. Ruby entered her with a finger, then another, stroking, curling, delving.

Yvonne exhaled sharply, rocking back against Ruby. She grabbed on to Ruby's waist, her breaths growing heavier and deeper. Still blindfolded, Ruby felt Yvonne's lips against her neck, then Yvonne's teeth against her shoulder, biting into her.

Suddenly, Yvonne's arms and thighs locked around Ruby, a near silent cry erupting from her as an orgasm overtook her. She pulsed around Ruby's fingers, gripping and releasing, until finally, she stiffened, then fell back against the pillows.

Ruby kissed her way up Yvonne's chest and neck. Yvonne let out a murmur, her hands on Ruby's cheeks, pushing the blindfold from Ruby's eyes. As she blinked against the lamplight, Ruby took in the sight of Yvonne's nude body. It hadn't escaped Ruby's notice that Yvonne had never stripped down before her, had never borne it all to Ruby, until now. Every inch of Yvonne's skin was as smooth as porcelain, all her curves perfectly round. Her nipples were a rosy brown that made Ruby want to kiss them again.

But before Ruby had the chance, Yvonne tossed the blindfold aside and let out a long breath. "Now I really am exhausted." She drew Ruby close. "Let's get some sleep."

Ruby nodded, then planted a soft kiss on Yvonne's lips, before turning onto her side and curling into the hollow made by her Mistress's body.

As she lay in the dark, pressed against Yvonne, Ruby's mind drifted back to their earlier conversation, which Yvonne had conveniently interrupted. Why was Yvonne so worried about Ruby meeting her family?

How bad could they be?

CHAPTER 19

Yvonne and Ruby pulled up in front of Yvonne's family home. Yvonne parked the car next to her brother's obnoxious red Ferrari. She'd opted to drive them herself rather than hiring a car service in the hope that she'd find it relaxing. It hadn't helped her relax one bit.

She got out of the car and opened the trunk. As she grabbed their overnight bags, Ruby appeared beside her.

"We've got this, Yvonne," she said. "Everything is going to be fine. We've got this."

Yvonne shut the trunk. "Let's get this over with."

They headed to the door. Yvonne unlocked it. She was always surprised that her key still worked. As they entered the house, a butler took their coats and overnight bags. Yvonne instructed him to take their things to her bedroom, breezing past him before he could insist on escorting them to the sitting room like they were guests. Yvonne wasn't a guest. This had been her home since she was born, long before her father had married her stepmother. Although

Alice owned it now, Yvonne wasn't going to let her stepmother treat her like she wasn't part of the family.

They reached the sitting room where Nicholas and her stepmother were waiting. The blonde-haired woman rose gracefully from her chair, greeting them with outspread arms.

"Yvonne, good to see you." She gave Yvonne a half-hearted hug before kissing the air next to her cheek.

"Hello, Alice," Yvonne replied. She nodded in her brother's direction. He hadn't bothered to get up. "Nicholas."

"Yvonne." He shot Ruby a smile. "We meet again, Ruby."

Before Ruby could respond, Alice turned her attention to her. "So, you're Ruby." Alice gave her the same awkward hug and kiss she'd given Yvonne. "It's lovely to meet you. Why don't you both have a seat? Dinner will be ready soon. Would you like something to drink?"

As Alice called for refreshments, Yvonne couldn't help but feel like something was off. It wasn't that Alice was being polite and friendly. Alice was always polite at first before the backhanded comments started.

"So," Alice began. "It's true. You're really married."

"That's right," Yvonne said.

"Well, it's a bit late, but congratulations. I hear it was something of a spontaneous event?"

"Yes, it was." Yvonne didn't elaborate.

"Now, Yvonne, don't be short with me." Alice crossed her ankles and folded her hands neatly in her lap. "I want to know the details. How did the two of you meet? When did you decide to get married?"

Yvonne sighed. *Here we go again.*

But before she could speak, Ruby put her hand on Yvonne's knee and gave her a look that said, *let me handle this.*

Yvonne gave her an almost imperceptible nod and sat back. Ruby began telling the story of how they'd 'met' years ago, with Yvonne adding the occasional detail. Madison's wedding had proved that Ruby was much more convincing when it came to telling people about their 'marriage.' She had a knack for it.

"Then, we both realized we wanted to be together for good," Ruby said. "So we thought, why wait? And that's how we ended up in a chapel in Vegas saying our vows in front of an Elvis impersonator." Somehow, Ruby made the story sound charming.

Alice gave her a wide smile. "Isn't that lovely? I'm so happy for you."

Yvonne held back a frown. That was it? No questions? No judgment? Usually, Alice didn't hold back her criticism of Yvonne. This was a woman who, when Yvonne was growing up, had insisted that the family get two sets of family photos taken, one with all four of them and one without Yvonne. Why was Alice being civil and polite now? And Nicholas hadn't said anything at all. Why wasn't he trying to poke holes in her story?

Was Yvonne being unfair to them both? After all, Yvonne wasn't exactly objective when it came to Alice or Nicholas, for a number of reasons. Their treatment of Yvonne as a child. The circumstances of Alice and Yvonne's father's marriage. It wouldn't be wrong to say Yvonne had always resented them. Yet, here they were, being kind to her. Alice had even congratulated her. Was her stepmother actually being genuine?

Ruby smiled at her. *See,* her eyes seemed to say. *Nothing to worry about.*

After half an hour of small talk, they went into the dining room for dinner, a formal multi-course affair at Alice's insistence. As they ate and made small talk, the atmosphere remained pleasant and civil. Although Nicholas didn't speak much, Alice seemed to be making an effort to get to know Ruby.

As they finished off the main course, Alice addressed Ruby. "Do you do anything for work?"

Ruby's mouth was full, so she couldn't answer immediately. Yvonne glanced at her stepmother. There was something odd about the smile plastered on her face. Yvonne looked at her brother. His face wore the same expression.

Suddenly, Yvonne was aware of an eerie stillness in the room.

"She used to be a waitress," Yvonne interjected. "But for now, she's settling into her new life here."

"Don't be rude, Yvonne," Alice said. "I asked Ruth, not you."

"That's basically it," Ruby said. "I was a waitress back in Vegas. I'm not sure what I'm going to do now though." She looked at Yvonne. "I haven't talked to Yvonne about it yet, but I'm thinking of going to culinary school."

Yvonne barely heard her. *Ruth.* Alice had called Ruby 'Ruth.' Her stomach turned to ice. She looked from her brother to her stepmother.

They knew.

That was why they'd been behaving so kindly. This

whole thing was a trap. Her brother and stepmother had just been waiting for the right moment to spring it.

She needed to get ahead of this.

Yvonne crossed her arms. "You can drop the act. If you have something to say to Ruby and me, say it."

Alice gave her a disdainful look. "Yvonne, these outbursts of yours aren't very ladylike."

"Don't play games with me, Alice. You called Ruby 'Ruth'. Neither of us has told you her real name. What, you did a background check on her? Went digging around in her life?"

Alice brought her hand to her chest, feigning offense. "I would never-"

"Yvonne's right," Nicholas said. "It's time to drop the act. Yes, I had a background check done on Ruby. What I found was very illuminating. We were giving you the opportunity to come clean, but you insist on keeping up this charade."

Yvonne looked at him blankly. "What charade?"

"Ruby isn't a waitress." Nicholas crossed his arms triumphantly. "She's an escort." When Yvonne showed no outward reaction, his expression darkened. "Don't you have anything to say? And don't try to deny it."

"I'm not going to deny it," Yvonne said.

"So you're admitting it?" Nicholas sputtered. "You married an escort to get Father's money?"

"I didn't say that."

"What-" Nicholas took a deep breath. "But you just admitted Ruby is an escort."

"She is. That's how we met. She was also a waitress until recently, but she gave both up on account of marrying me. It would hardly be fitting for my wife to continue her previous occupation now that we're in a committed relationship."

Nicholas looked from Ruby to Yvonne. "Do you seriously expect me to believe the two of you are in a relationship?"

"It's the truth."

"Really, Yvonne?" Alice said. "Did you actually think such a desperate farce would work? Did you think you could make us believe you fell in love with this woman?" She gestured dismissively at Ruby.

"I don't see why it's so hard to believe."

Nicholas scoffed. "While I've heard all about your twisted sexual tendencies, you would never enter a relationship with some Vegas prostitute. This is obviously a plot to get your hands on Father's money. On *my* money."

Yvonne spoke with an icy calm. "You're very much mistaken. Firstly, that money is mine, not yours. Secondly, Ruby is *not* a prostitute."

Nicholas turned to Ruby, his lips twisting up into a fake smile. "I'm sorry, it's hard to keep up with which terms are politically correct these days. What do you prefer to be called? A call girl? A hooker? A *whore*?"

Yvonne rose from her seat, planting her fists on the table before her. "Say another word about Ruby, and I will *end* you."

Yvonne glared at him, her fists clenched and her body tense. It was taking all her effort not to unleash the full force of her anger on him.

Nicholas smirked. "I don't see what the problem is. I'm just being honest." He turned to Ruby. "That's what you escorts do, isn't it? Whore yourselves out for money? How much is she paying you to fuck her?"

Rage boiled up inside Yvonne. Before she could say a word, she felt Ruby's hand on hers.

"It's okay, Yvonne," Ruby said. "You don't need to defend me."

"Yes, I do." Yvonne took in a breath, steadying herself. "So what if Ruby is an escort? That doesn't make her any less deserving of your respect. Ruby is my wife. We are in a committed relationship. You need to respect that."

For what had to be the first time ever, Alice looked cowed.

Nicholas, however, did not. "I don't believe you for a second." He scoffed. "You're so desperate, you had to pay someone to marry you? In ten years, you couldn't even find someone who actually wanted to be with you. You're pathetic."

Next to her, Ruby began to speak.

But Yvonne cut her off. "I will not sit here while you insult me and my wife." She looked at Ruby. "We're done here."

She grabbed Ruby's hand, dragged her out of her seat, and marched out of the room.

∼

Yvonne pulled Ruby into the bedroom and shut the door. Their bags were by the bed, so Ruby assumed the room was Yvonne's bedroom. There was little else to indicate the room belonged to her. It was sparse and impersonal, the only remnant of Yvonne's childhood a small stuffed bear on a shelf in the corner.

Yvonne sat down on the bed, her body stiff and tense.

Ruby joined her. "Are you okay? Things got pretty heated in there."

"I'm fine," Yvonne replied. "It wouldn't be a family dinner if it didn't end in a verbal brawl between Nicholas and me." She leaned back and crossed her legs. "Are you all right? I'm sorry about my brother. I can't believe he had the nerve to say those things to you."

"I'm fine. I've been called worse before. It comes with the job."

"I apologize for subjecting you to this. We never should have come here. We should leave."

"Is that a good idea? It's getting late." The drive would be dangerous in the dark.

"You're right. We can leave first thing in the morning." Yvonne rubbed her temples. "Coming here is always tough. There are so many memories here. Very few of them are good ones."

Her gaze flicked over to the nightstand. Ruby followed the path of Yvonne's eyes to a framed photo on top of it. Yvonne reached over and picked it up. The faded picture was of a young woman with the same dark wavy hair as Yvonne, holding an adorably chubby toddler in a frilly dress.

"Is that you?" Ruby asked.

Yvonne nodded. "My mother and me. It was taken a few months before she died. I was three. It was a car accident."

"I'm sorry. That must have been awful."

"I don't remember it, really. I have very few memories of

her. Most of them are so vague and muddled that I don't even know if they're real. But someone has to remember her. Everyone else seems determined to forget she ever existed. Even when he was alive, my father wanted to forget her, probably out of guilt."

"What do you mean?"

"My brother, Nicholas. He was born exactly nine months after my mother died."

Ruby frowned. "Are you saying…"

"I'm saying, either my father barely waited until my mother's funeral before he started fucking his secretary, or he'd been cheating on her long before she died. I've always suspected the latter. It would explain why he tried so hard to erase her, and why he resented me. I was a reminder of the woman he betrayed."

"Your father resented you?"

"He never said anything, but it was obvious. He wasn't kind to me, growing up. And his new family—Alice, and Nicholas—they took their cues from him, treating me with the same hostility. I was the unwanted stepchild. It didn't help that I didn't look anything like the rest of my pale, blonde-haired family." Yvonne's voice wavered slightly. "I spent my entire childhood feeling like I wasn't really part of my family."

"Oh, Yvonne. I'm so sorry. I can't believe anyone could be so cruel to their own family."

Yvonne placed the photo aside onto the bed. "I wasn't family. Not to them."

Ruby put a comforting hand on Yvonne's arm. So much about the woman Ruby called her Mistress was starting to make sense. She would have had to grow a thick skin to endure such a painful childhood. But did her icy exterior serve another purpose? Was it to hide the pain of loneliness, of feeling unwanted? Was it to keep others from getting close enough to reject her, just like her own family had?

"It wasn't all bad," Yvonne said. "I still had one person I could call family."

Ruby recalled what Yvonne had told her that night after the wedding. "You mean your nanny. Nita."

Yvonne nodded. "She and my mother were close, despite the fact that Nita worked for her. After my mother's passing, Nita was the only person in my life who acknowledged her existence. She told me stories of my mother, taught me how to cook all her favorite dishes. She kept the memory of my mother alive for me.

"But it was so much more than that. In erasing my mother, my father also erased any connection I had with my Chinese heritage, my mother's culture. Having that part of myself ignored and unacknowledged was so isolating. Nita, she helped me connect with that part of myself. She made sure I didn't grow up feeling like I didn't belong anywhere, made sure I knew I had a place, both in the world and with her. I'll always be grateful for that."

"She really means a lot to you, doesn't she?" Ruby said. "That's why you're going through so much trouble to get the money for her."

"Yes. I owe it to her."

"That's sweet of you."

"I'm simply repaying her for helping me, that's all," Yvonne said. "I'll breathe easier once this money comes through and everything is sorted for her for good. Nicholas finding out the truth puts a wrench in the works."

"It's not like he has any proof. And you said all we need is a witness who will say our marriage is genuine. We have plenty of those, especially after the wedding."

"That's true."

Ruby smiled. "We're doing a great job at this whole marriage thing. We make a good couple."

"You're right. We do." Yvonne picked up the photo and returned it to its place on the nightstand, then turned back to Ruby. "So, you want to go to culinary school, do you?"

"Right." In the chaos that dinner had descended into, Ruby had forgotten she'd said anything about it. "I was only half serious. I like baking, but I'm not very good at it, so it could be fun to learn how to do it properly. And, when I was a kid, I had this dream of opening my own bakery." She looked down at her lap, shaking her head. "I always thought it was silly. But right now, the idea doesn't seem so silly."

Yvonne took Ruby's chin, tilting Ruby's head up to look into her eyes. "It's not silly at all. If it makes you happy, you should do it." She leaned in and gave Ruby a brief kiss.

Ruby's heart fluttered, the tenderness in Yvonne's lips unexpected. She'd gotten that same fluttery feeling when Yvonne had stuck up for her at dinner. She didn't need anyone to defend her. She could hold her own.

But it felt good, knowing that Yvonne had her back. Ruby was starting to see that her Mistress had a softer side. Hearing Yvonne speak of her mother, her childhood, filled Ruby with emotion. She'd never seen Yvonne so naked and vulnerable.

Ruby couldn't deny it any longer. The feelings she harbored for Yvonne, they went far beyond what she should feel for a client. She was losing herself in Yvonne, and it scared her. Ruby didn't want to feel the things she felt for Yvonne. Not when everything between them was so complicated. Not when Ruby had been here before, with someone so like Yvonne, and had gotten hurt, badly.

But Yvonne was nothing like *him*. Yvonne wouldn't hurt her.

Could it be different this time?

CHAPTER 20

Yvonne raked her eyes along Ruby's body. Ruby was stretched out across the playroom bed, clothed, for now, in a loose, casual dress. Her wrists were handcuffed to the headboard above her, and she was lying on her stomach, her head turned to the side, looking up at Yvonne expectantly.

Yvonne flicked the flogger she was holding against her palm, to Ruby's obvious delight. After returning from Yvonne's stressful family dinner, they'd both felt the need to blow off some steam.

And what better way to do that than this?

"What should I do with you?" Yvonne drew the flogger up the back of Ruby's thigh, letting its many tails trail over the other woman's skin. "Now that I have you bound and at my mercy, I'm overwhelmed by all the possibilities." She let the tails of the flogger slip between Ruby's thighs. "Should I keep you on the edge, denying you release until you beg me to allow you to come? Or should I make you come over and over and over until you beg me to stop?"

Ruby said nothing, but a red flush crept up her cheeks.

"I'm in the mood for a little delayed gratification." Yvonne dragged the back of Ruby's skirt up her thighs. "On your end, that is. This is going to be immensely satisfying for me."

Ruby buried her face in the pillow before her. Yvonne gave Ruby's ass a testing flick with the flogger, eliciting a shudder from Ruby. Yvonne relished Ruby's reactions. She wanted to spend the entire night getting lost with Ruby, forgetting about the rest of the world and all her problems.

But it was hard for her to forget about her problems when her biggest problem was Ruby herself.

Ruby. Her submissive. Her 'wife'. But she was so much more than that to Yvonne. And it was becoming impossible for Yvonne to ignore that fact.

Ruby peered back at her. Presumably, she thought the delay was because Yvonne wanted to torment her, as usual. Did she have any idea of the battle going on in Yvonne's mind? Did she realize how much she was tormenting Yvonne?

Did Ruby feel the same way Yvonne did?

Yvonne pushed the thought aside. "No peeking."

Ruby bit her lip. "I just…"

"Well? What is it?"

"Nothing." She buried her face in the pillow again.

"Oh? Don't tell me you've gotten shy all of a sudden." Yvonne drew the flogger along Ruby's ass cheek before giving it another flick. "Don't pretend you don't want this."

As Yvonne raised the flogger again, the air in the room iced over. She paused. A moment ago, Ruby had been squirming on the bed with anticipation. Now, her body was stiff, and she was breathing hard. A chill washed over Yvonne.

Something was very wrong.

She dropped the flogger and put her hand on Ruby's shoulder. "Ruby?"

Ruby's voice was so quiet Yvonne could barely hear her. "Get these off me."

The cuffs. "All right. Stay calm."

Yvonne grabbed the key to the handcuffs from the top drawer of the nightstand and unlocked the cuffs around Ruby's wrists. Ruby sat up, pulling her hands in close to her and curling her legs up to her chin.

"Ruby, are you okay?"

Ruby looked up at her, her eyes vacant and quivering. "I thought…"

"You thought what?" Yvonne kept her outward demeanor as calm as possible for Ruby's sake. "Ruby, what is it?"

"I thought you weren't going to let me go."

Yvonne flinched. "Why would you think that? Ruby, I would never, ever, ever do anything like that."

"I know." Ruby shook her head repeatedly, as though she were trying to shake free a thought. "I know. It was stupid, I know you're not *him*, I just…"

"Him?" Yvonne put a hand on Ruby's arm. "Ruby, what's going on?"

Ruby pulled away, her eyes downcast. "It's nothing."

"Ruby, talk to me. Who do you mean?"

"I don't want to talk about it."

Yvonne stifled a curse. Ruby was shutting down on her. That was the worst thing that could happen right now, given that Ruby had been in such a vulnerable state moments ago. She'd be feeling raw and emotional. If Yvonne didn't do something soon, things would get much worse. But it was impossible for her to do anything when she didn't know what was going on.

Yvonne changed tack. "You don't have to tell me what's going on. Just tell me what you need from me right now."

"I just want to be alone," Ruby said.

Yvonne shook her head. "Ruby, you need to understand, you can't be alone right now. You're not yourself. You're having some kind of reaction to what we were doing. Ending a scene like this, so abruptly, it means you're going to crash. You need aftercare. You need me." She looked into Ruby's eyes, pleading with her. "Let me help you."

"I'm sorry," Ruby said, her voice shaking. "I just, I can't."

Without another word, Ruby got up from the bed and fled the room.

A flood of dread consumed Yvonne. She wanted to go after Ruby, but Ruby had made herself clear. She sat down on the edge of the bed. She felt so helpless.

Not a minute later, she heard the front door slam shut.

Ruby was gone.

~

Ruby wandered through the park absently. She'd been walking aimlessly for who knew how long now. She didn't know what she was doing or where she was going. It wasn't like she had anywhere to go in this stupid city. She'd just felt the urge to escape that tiny room, that apartment.

She steadied herself. Her thoughts were spiraling,

along with her emotions. It hadn't taken long for the initial fear she'd felt to pass, but it had been replaced with a deep gnawing within her, like she was being eaten from inside.

Ruby collapsed onto a nearby bench. She felt awful about how she'd reacted toward Yvonne. Ruby hadn't truly believed Yvonne would hurt her. Yvonne's actions tonight had made that even more clear. Ruby hadn't even used her safeword, but Yvonne had stopped anyway.

Yvonne wasn't *him*. Ruby knew that. But at that moment, when Yvonne had said those words, she'd gone right back to that nightmare of her past, a past she'd thought she'd finally overcome.

But she just couldn't escape it.

She swallowed back her growing tears. Her thoughts were going to dark places. What was wrong with her? Was this that 'crash' Yvonne had warned her about, that drop that came after the high? Her emotions felt out of control.

Yvonne had been right. Ruby needed her. But she didn't think she was capable of walking home without collapsing into a puddle of sobs.

Her hands trembling, she took out her phone and called Yvonne.

Yvonne picked up instantly. "Ruby. Where are you?"

There was something comforting about Yvonne's firm, steady voice. Ruby couldn't stop her own voice from quivering when she finally spoke. "I'm at the park."

"I'll be right there. Don't go anywhere. I won't be long."

Ruby hung up the phone. All she had to do was keep it together until Yvonne arrived, but the prospect seemed impossible. She felt so miserable and alone. She was glad there was no one else around. It was taking all her effort to keep the despair she felt from overwhelming her.

Yvonne arrived five minutes later, but it felt like so much longer. As soon as she spotted Ruby, she hurried over and pulled Ruby into her arms. The next thing Ruby knew, she was sobbing uncontrollably.

"You were right." A tremor went through her. "I'm so sorry."

"It's okay," Yvonne held her tightly. "I'm here. You're all right."

"Why do I feel like this? I've never felt so awful before."

"I know. It's just subdrop. You'll start to feel better soon. Why don't we go home so I can take care of you?"

Ruby sniffled. "I think I need a minute."

"That's okay. We have all the time in the world."

Yvonne pulled Ruby down to sit on the bench, drawing her close again. Ruby closed her eyes and buried herself in Yvonne's shoulder, letting everything she was feeling flow from her. Eventually, her tears dried up, and she stopped shaking, but she was still left with a hollow, sinking feeling in her chest.

She pulled away. "I'm so sorry for how I acted."

"You don't need to apologize," Yvonne said.

"I didn't mean it. It wasn't you that I was running away from. I don't think you'd ever do anything to hurt me."

"I know. And we don't need to talk about this now. It can wait till later."

"But I *do* want to talk about it," Ruby said.

"Are you sure? All your emotions are heightened right now. It isn't the best time to talk about something sensitive."

"I'm sure. I need to tell you the truth." Ruby drew in a

slow, deep breath. "There's something I've been keeping from you."

Yvonne was silent for a moment. "Is this about 'him?'"

Ruby nodded. "He was a client. At least, he was at first. Then he became more."

"You were in a relationship with him?"

"Yes. But not just any relationship." Ruby hesitated. "He was my Dom."

Yvonne's lips tightened, a visible flash of anger behind her eyes.

"I know! All along, you thought I was new to this, and I let you think that. I lied to you, even after you told me over and over how important it was for us to be honest with each other. I'm sorry. I messed up, and I know it."

"Ruby, it's not you that I'm mad at. This man, this so-called 'Dom.' He mistreated you, didn't he?"

"Not at first." Ruby's voice faltered. "When I started seeing him as a client, he seemed so charming and kind. We clicked instantly. I've been doing the escort thing for a long time, and until then I'd never had feelings for a client, let alone considered a relationship with one. So many clients tried to win me over, to 'save' me, to buy me away from my life of escorting.

"But he wasn't like that at all. He seemed so genuine. And I was so drawn to the power he radiated, even before he told me he was a Dom. I've always had a submissive side, but I'd never truly explored it until him. The more we explored together, the harder I fell for him, until eventually, I realized I was in love with him. So when he asked me to move in with him, to be his girlfriend and submissive, and to give up my job, I agreed. Everything was great at first. But it didn't take long before things began to change."

Ruby swallowed. "He wasn't like you. He wasn't careful. He didn't care about safewords and limits, let alone aftercare. He said we didn't need any of that. He said that we trusted each other, and that was all that mattered. And I believed him, until he…"

Yvonne put her hand on Ruby's. "You don't need to talk about this if you don't want to."

"No, I do." Ruby drew in a deep breath. "It started when he became controlling in subtle ways, with small, mundane things. He'd dictate what I was allowed to do, how I was allowed to dress, all in a way that made it seem like it was part of our power games. I didn't think anything of it at the time. Then, he started crossing lines in a physical way. He'd push my limits, do things he knew I didn't like, and he'd apologize after. But then he started taking things even further. He wouldn't listen when I said no, wouldn't stop when I said stop."

She cast her eyes down, not wanting to face Yvonne's reaction. "He never forced himself on me in the typical sense. It was everything else that he'd take too far. He'd hurt me, or he'd keep me tied up when I wanted him to let me go. And when I protested, he'd tell me that I wanted him to do those things, that I'd asked for it. It made me doubt myself. I'd wanted all those things, hadn't I? So I couldn't complain when he was just doing what I wanted, what I'd agreed to. And most of the time, everything else between us was good, so I just let his treatment of me slide."

"Oh, Ruby." Yvonne's voice trembled.

"I know that he was manipulating me, abusing me, but

back then it was so hard to see it. I'd just become this shell of a person, this empty, formless vessel with no desires of my own. I became nothing more than what he wanted me to be."

Ruby's hands curled into fists. "I don't remember exactly when I came to my senses, I just remember this moment when I looked into his eyes, and I realized there was no love in them. I realized that if he loved me, he wouldn't hurt me. I realized that I was just a *thing* to him, someone he could use for his own sick, twisted needs. So I left him."

Yvonne took Ruby's hand and squeezed it. "I'm so sorry he did that to you. He wasn't a Dominant, he was an abusive, evil person. No Dominant would treat their submissive that way."

"I know that, now. But after what he did, it made it hard for me to trust anyone with my heart, with my body, with any part of me. That side of me that craved submission was still there, but I couldn't imagine ever submitting to anyone else again."

Ruby looked up at Yvonne. "Not until you. Since then, you're the first person I've felt able to be vulnerable with. I don't know why, but from the moment we met, I felt like I could trust you. And now I've screwed everything up."

"You haven't screwed anything up," Yvonne said. "I understand why you got upset tonight. I can see how what we were doing hit too close to home. I should have been more careful."

"No, it was on me. I was distracted. I was thinking about him, about everything I went through with him." Ruby didn't mention that the reason her former client had been on her mind was that she was worrying about falling for a client again. "And then, when you said those words that reminded me of what he used to say, it threw me, and suddenly I couldn't handle it. I'm sorry."

"Don't be. And thank you for opening up to me about this. I wish you'd told me sooner, but I understand that it must be difficult to talk about."

Ruby shook her head. "That's not why I kept this from you. It's not that I find it hard to talk about. It's because you're so careful about everything we're doing together. You take it all so seriously, and you trusted me to be honest and open with you, but I thought that if you knew the truth, you'd want to end what we were doing. You were already so reluctant to do this with me, and you were so afraid of hurting me. You said so yourself, that night when I found your playroom." Ruby's voice faltered. "I was afraid that if you knew about what I'd been through, you'd think I was too broken for this."

"Ruby." Yvonne stared at her. "How could I ever think you were broken? Sometimes you're so perfect, I don't know what to do with you."

"So you don't want to end things between us? You don't want to stop what we're doing?"

Yvonne was silent for a moment. "Perhaps we should take a step back."

"Please don't say that! Yvonne, being your submissive has meant so much to me. You've shown me what it's like to have a Dominant who really cares. I always knew that was how it was supposed to be, but I'd never experienced it. It doesn't matter that our relationship is just an arrangement. You've shown me that I can trust someone with my desires, and that you won't break that trust. I've always found joy in submission, in serving, but he took that from me. You've helped me reclaim that part of myself. You gave me a safe haven to pick up all the pieces of my life. That means the world to me." Ruby's voice caught in her throat. "I don't want to lose what we have. I don't want to lose *you*."

Yvonne took Ruby's cheek in her hand. "You won't. I promise you. But we need to change how we approach things. We need to be more careful, more open and honest. Both of us."

Ruby nodded. "Okay."

"There's something I need you to do for me," Yvonne said. "When you feel ready, I want you to write down something you want me to do with you, something you want more than anything else. Your deepest, most hidden desire."

Ruby shook her head. "There's nothing I want from you that you don't already give me. And I like it when you take the lead."

"No," Yvonne said. "This is about you, not me. You're going to have to take the lead for once. You're going to have to tell me what you want. Once you figure it out, sit down and write it down for me. Be specific and detailed."

Ruby frowned. "Why do I feel like you're giving me homework?"

A slight smile crossed Yvonne's lips. "I suppose I am. And for good measure, there will be no more games between us until then."

Ruby sighed. "Okay."

Yvonne squeezed Ruby's shoulder. "Are you ready to go home? We'll take a nice long bath, then cuddle up in my bed together. How does that sound?"

Ruby smiled. "That sounds perfect."

As they left the park and headed toward home, the anxiety in Ruby's stomach turned to butterflies. She'd definitely fallen for Yvonne.

But was it possible that Yvonne, a woman so guarded with her heart, felt the same way Ruby did?

CHAPTER 21

Yvonne stood in her darkened living room. It was late at night, and she'd just arrived home as silently as possible. Ruby was in her bedroom waiting for Yvonne, just like Yvonne had told her to an hour ago. That was plenty of time to get her all worked up for what was to come.

Ruby had done her 'homework'. She'd written down exactly what she wanted from Yvonne. Tonight, they were going to live out Ruby's fantasy.

And it left Yvonne feeling unsettled.

It wasn't that she felt uncomfortable with what Ruby was asking of her, or that she had any reservations about continuing their Dominant/submissive relationship. They were being extra careful. After the other night, Yvonne had given Ruby a long lecture about limits, trust, the importance of communication, including using her safeword.

Yvonne wasn't taking any chances. She'd made sure Ruby knew she had outs, and she was prepared to call things off at the first sign of trouble. She was confident that Ruby wouldn't try to push herself further than she could handle. She trusted Ruby when she said that this was what she wanted.

No, the reason Yvonne was nervous was because she'd never, *ever* let a submissive have so much control. She'd never given a submissive the freedom to dictate terms. While Yvonne always made sure her submissive's needs were met, it was on Yvonne's terms, not theirs.

But tonight, Ruby held the whip. Tonight, Yvonne was hers. And Yvonne wanted this.

That excited her as much as it scared her. Yvonne's insistence on always calling the shots was her way of keeping control of the situation. Her insistence on not bowing to her submissive's desires was a way to keep them at arm's length, just like everyone else in her life. Ruby was no exception.

What would it feel like to let Ruby in? That was the ultimate surrender, wasn't it? To let someone in, physically, mentally, emotionally? To give Ruby parts of herself she'd never given anyone else? She'd already come close to doing so more than once. It was just so easy with Ruby. She had this way of slipping under Yvonne's guard, of making her feel all the things she never allowed herself to feel, making her want things she'd never let herself want.

Yvonne didn't like feeling this way. It made her vulnerable, all the more likely to get hurt. Because that was what always happened in the end. People always hurt her.

It was easier to not let anyone in in the first place.

Yvonne took the sheet of paper Ruby had written her 'homework' on out of her pocket and unfolded it, scanning it once more. At first, Yvonne had been surprised by what Ruby wanted, but the more she thought about it, the more she understood. Ruby had had the joy of total submission stolen from her by someone who had taken advantage of her.

Tonight, Ruby wanted to take that back.

That Ruby trusted Yvonne enough to let this hidden fantasy of hers play out set Yvonne's heart alight. When she'd given Ruby this task, handing control over to her, Yvonne had simply seen it as a way to reestablish the trust between them. But Ruby was asking for something bigger than that, whether she knew it or not.

Ruby trusted Yvonne to do this with her and keep her safe, despite everything she'd been through, despite having her trust betrayed by someone before. It meant Yvonne had to be more careful. It meant she couldn't continue approaching their relationship as she had been, like it was a transaction with clearly defined rules. Rules meant nothing when emotions were involved. Emotions made it far easier for someone to get hurt.

And after everything Ruby had been through, how could there not be emotions involved in every interaction she had with Yvonne, whether it was as escort and client, or Dominant and submissive?

Yvonne folded up the piece of paper and returned it to her pocket. She'd left Ruby waiting long enough.

CHAPTER 22

The floorboards creaked outside Ruby's bedroom door. Her breath caught in her throat. Was her Mistress at the door, coming to give Ruby what she wanted more than anything?

She got up from the bed. "Yvonne?"

There was no answer.

Ruby crept to the door. Before she could open it, it flung open. She only had a second to register Yvonne's presence along with the leather bag she was holding before Yvonne dropped the bag to the floor, seized Ruby by the shoulders and pushed her hard against the wall beside the door.

Ruby gasped. "Y-"

Yvonne put a hand over Ruby's mouth. "Don't. Say. A word."

Ruby nodded slowly.

Yvonne shut the door beside her and locked it, before turning back to Ruby. Ruby's heart raced. The thirst in the other woman's eyes made their depths seem endless.

Suddenly, Yvonne spun Ruby around, pinning her against the wall with her body. Her breasts pressed into Ruby's back, her hot breath burning the side of Ruby's face.

"Don't speak," Yvonne growled softly. "Don't move. Don't do anything unless I tell you to."

Ruby shut her eyes, desire lighting her up from within. Yvonne grabbed Ruby's hip with one hand and slid the other inside the front of Ruby's panties, cupping her roughly between her thighs. Ruby drew in a long, slow breath. She'd never gotten so wet so quickly.

Yvonne spoke into Ruby's ear. "Tonight, you're all mine. Tonight, you're nothing other than my toy, my plaything. Do you understand?"

Ruby nodded. She was Yvonne's captive.

There was nothing she wanted more.

Yvonne dragged Ruby to the bed, tossing her onto it. Then she grabbed the leather bag and dropped it on the floor next to the bed, opening it up and producing several coils of rope.

She set them on the bed beside Ruby. "This is to make sure you can't go anywhere."

Yvonne grabbed Ruby's wrist and bound it to the bedpost at the top corner of the bed before starting on her other wrist. Ruby looked up at her wrist. The ropes binding it were heavy and rough, and the knots Yvonne had tied weren't the elaborate, decorative knots she'd used on Ruby in The Rope Room at Lilith's Den. They were functional, sturdy knots, serving no purpose other than to keep Ruby restrained.

Yvonne finished tying Ruby's other wrist to the bedpost.

With no warning or fanfare, she slid her hands down Ruby's sides and tore Ruby's panties from her legs, leaving scrapes behind on her thighs. Ruby's breath quickened, need welling up deep within her. She was still wearing her t-shirt, but she felt completely naked. The way Yvonne was looking down at her only made her feel more exposed.

Yvonne dangled Ruby's panties from her finger. "This is to make sure you can't use that sweet mouth of yours to try to talk your way out of this."

Yvonne balled Ruby's panties up in her hand and took Ruby's chin, prying her mouth open. Before she could process what was happening, Yvonne stuffed the panties in Ruby's mouth.

Ruby let out a muffled cry, dizzy from the scent and taste of her own arousal on her panties. Could she push out the gag with her tongue if she tried? Probably.

But that didn't make it any less exhilarating.

Yvonne picked up the remaining coils of rope from the bed and unwound them. Ruby lifted her head to watch, her shoulders straining against the ropes binding her to the bed. Noticing Ruby watching her, Yvonne grabbed Ruby's hair and pulled her head back down to the pillow.

"Stay down," Yvonne said. "If I have to blindfold you, I won't be happy."

Ruby gave a tiny nod. Yvonne got up from the bed and proceeded to tie Ruby's ankles to the bedposts, leaving her bound, spread-eagled, to the bed.

Ruby's pulse began to pound. She pulled at her bonds, adrenaline flooding her veins. She could use her safeword if she wanted to. She could signal to Yvonne to stop.

But the last thing Ruby wanted was to stop. She craved this, her most twisted fantasy, more than anything. This was her choice, and that made all the difference. She was in control. And with every moment that passed, her hunger only deepened.

Ruby glanced up at Yvonne looming above her. Yvonne still wore that ravenous expression, but the passion in her eyes hinted at the fact that her actions were motivated by something much tenderer.

She dipped down, her face less than an inch from Ruby's. "For the rest of the night, you will exist solely for my satisfaction. If I choose to permit you pleasure, it will be for my enjoyment only." She drew a line up the front of Ruby's thigh with a fingernail, leaving a trail of pink behind on Ruby's skin. "And I intend to enjoy this. I intend to enjoy *you*."

The icy calm in Yvonne's voice sent a chill rolling down the length of Ruby's body. She pulled at the ropes binding her even harder, but they didn't budge. All the while, the need within her grew.

Yvonne ran her hands up Ruby's stomach, pushing her t-shirt upward. "This is getting in my way."

Yvonne returned to the leather bag and withdrew a pair of scissors. She brandished them before Ruby, giving her a look that froze her in place. Ruby lay dead still as Yvonne took the bottom hem of Ruby's t-shirt and snipped through it, the back of the cold metal blade skimming across her skin. Yvonne sliced through the t-shirt from top to bottom and at the shoulders, before ripping it from Ruby's body entirely.

Ruby quivered, her bare nipples peaking. Yvonne placed the scissors aside and crawled onto the bed, straddling her.

"That's better," Yvonne said. "Now, where was I?"

She traced her hands over Ruby's chest, her fingertips skating over a nipple, before pinching it, hard. Ruby sucked in a breath, her chest bucking. Yvonne dipped down to take Ruby's nipple with her mouth. A groan spilled from Ruby's lips. The feel of Yvonne's wet tongue and lips against her swollen bud was so exquisite. At the same time, Yvonne drew her hand up to pinch Ruby's other nipple. Ruby cried out through her gag, pure, concentrated pleasure lancing through her.

A murmur rose from Yvonne's chest. "The sounds you make are so delicious. I could listen to them all night. I could do this all night, make you scream, over and over." She fixed her eyes on Ruby's. "And since I have you bound and at my mercy, that's exactly what I'm going to do to you."

Ruby shuddered, the hairs standing up on her skin. It was clear that Yvonne meant her threat. Yvonne grazed her lips down the side of Ruby's neck, biting her shoulder, causing Ruby to moan. She grabbed a fistful of Ruby's hair, tugging it firmly, coaxing a pleasured hiss from Ruby. She raked her fingers down Ruby's front, leaving faint red lines on her breasts and stomach.

All the while, Ruby squirmed and bucked, the panties muffling every sound she made. Pleasure? Pain? She couldn't tell the difference anymore. It was all so exquisite. She was intoxicated by it all, and by Yvonne, her Mistress. She wanted Yvonne to take her, claim her, use her until she was Yvonne's so completely that all her edges dissolved away and the two of them became one.

"That's it," Yvonne said. "Surrender to me."

As Yvonne continued to ravish her, Ruby closed her eyes, letting herself fall into a familiar trance of submission. She relaxed into the flow, trusting that Yvonne wouldn't hurt her, that she would keep Ruby safe, no matter how vulnerable she was.

As she let go, all the sensations she was feeling amplified. The pressure and roughness of the ropes binding her wrists and ankles. Yvonne's scent, a perfume tailor-made to make Ruby weak. Yvonne's fingers, pinching and scratching and teasing Ruby's sensitive skin. The satin of Yvonne's lips as she assailed every inch of Ruby's body with them.

Yvonne slid her hand between Ruby's thighs, dragging her fingers over Ruby's folds. "You're so wet. So ready for me."

Ruby quivered. Yvonne pushed a finger inside her. It slipped in easily, piercing deep, but not deep enough. Ruby held back a whimper.

Yvonne drew away. "I'm ready for you too."

She got up from the bed. Ruby watched silently as Yvonne pulled her blouse over her head and stepped out of her pants. But it wasn't just a bra and panties she wore underneath. Her black boyleg briefs, embellished with lace, doubled as a harness that held a black dildo.

Ruby bit her lip. She'd felt something hard at her back when Yvonne had pushed her against the wall earlier, but she'd been too distracted for it to register. Now, the dildo was impossible to miss.

"You have no idea how long I've been waiting to fuck you properly," Yvonne said.

Ruby inhaled sharply, heat flooding her core. Yvonne

rearranged the panty harness, pulling it up at the waistband, before crawling back onto the bed and positioning herself between Ruby's outspread legs.

Ruby's breath grew slow and heavy. Yvonne took the dildo in one hand and guided it into Ruby's slit, entering her with one push. Ruby cried out, ecstasy surging through her. Yvonne buried herself inside her, over and over, deep and unhesitating. She clutched at Ruby's waist, her fingers digging into Ruby's skin.

Ruby let out a moan, the panties in her mouth soaked through. She watched Yvonne grinding and rocking on top of her, hypnotized by the dark-haired goddess who had claimed her. Yvonne rolled her hips harder, penetrating Ruby deeper, holding her tighter. Ruby writhed, breathless, straining against her bonds, fighting the unbearable throbbing inside.

As Yvonne thrust inside her, Ruby's pleasure reached a peak. She strained against her bonds as the force of her climax ripped through her. She shattered underneath her Mistress, the euphoria of her complete and utter surrender almost too much to bear.

But even as Ruby's orgasm passed, Yvonne didn't stop. She pulled back slightly, shifting her weight, her pace and rhythm changing. She rocked her hips back and forth, one hand on the bed to steady herself, and the other on Ruby's chest, until at last, her head fell back, and she let out a wild, trembling cry.

Yvonne stilled, her eyes closed, her breathing firm and heavy. It only took a moment for her to recover. She reached down and cradled the curve of Ruby's cheek.

"Had enough?" Yvonne asked.

Ruby nodded. She'd reached a state of such perfect bliss that she couldn't possibly take anymore.

Gently, Yvonne pulled the panties from Ruby's mouth. For the first time that night, Yvonne leaned down and pressed her lips to Ruby's in a tender but possessive kiss, sending gentle ripples through Ruby's whole body. Ruby shut her eyes, melting into her Mistress.

After a moment, Yvonne drew back and untied Ruby's ankles and wrists. Ruby was free. The spell had been lifted.

But she was still Yvonne's captive.

She looked up at Yvonne, her eyes watering, her chest brimming with emotion. "Yvonne," she whispered. "Mistress."

Yvonne gazed back at her. "My beautiful, precious Ruby."

Yvonne gathered Ruby into her arms and held her so close that she couldn't tell where she ended and Yvonne began.

∼

Yvonne glanced at Ruby. She was still passed out on the bed beside Yvonne, so still that the only sign of life she gave off was the satisfied expression on her face.

Yvonne felt the same way. It was surprising. She didn't usually go for those kinds of rough games. Although she had no objection to them, she simply preferred more subtle kinds of force, power that wasn't physical.

Yet, Yvonne had found tonight even more gratifying than anything else she and Ruby had ever done together.

Ruby blew out a soft sigh, her eyes flickering open.

Noticing Yvonne's gaze on her, her cheeks turned pink, but she smiled.

"How are you feeling?" Yvonne asked

"Incredible," Ruby murmured.

Yvonne returned her smile, but felt exhaustion pressing on her. Her entire body ached, and she felt raw, not in an unpleasant way, but in an unfamiliar way. Perhaps Madison had been right. There was a certain vulnerability in holding the whip too.

Ruby sat up, folding her legs underneath her. "So, now that you've done something for me, is there anything I can do for you?"

Yvonne thought for a moment. Perhaps it wasn't a bad idea to let Ruby take care of her, just this once. "I could use a massage."

"Sure. Anything you want, Mistress."

Yvonne rolled onto her stomach and folded her arms beneath her head. Immediately, Ruby began kneading Yvonne's shoulders with surprising firmness. Yvonne let out a contented moan. Ruby's hands felt heavenly.

"Is that good?" Ruby asked.

"So good," Yvonne murmured. "Don't stop."

Yvonne sank into the bed. As her physical aches eased, the deeper, vaguer ache within her only grew. Something was gnawing at her. Why had she found tonight so satisfying? There was a simple explanation.

It was because tonight, she'd made Ruby happy.

Yvonne hadn't realized, until now, how much she cherished Ruby's happiness. She'd never felt this way about anyone before.

"Yvonne?" Ruby said.

Yvonne returned to reality. "Yes?"

"I want to say thank you. For tonight."

"You don't have to thank me," Yvonne murmured. "I wouldn't have done any of this if I didn't want to."

"Yes, but you didn't have to do what you did. You didn't have to give me this. We could have just kept doing everything like we used to. But you did all this, for me, and then you held me in your arms, and kissed me, and made sure I was okay afterward."

"I'm your Domme," Yvonne said. "That's just my job."

Ruby pulled her hands away. "No, it's not."

"Yes, it *is*." Yvonne turned over and sat up. "I know your past experiences weren't great, but-"

"This isn't about that." Ruby crossed her arms. "I already told you, I know that ex-client of mine was wrong in the way he treated me. I know that a real Dominant takes care of their submissive. Do you think I'm so damaged that I'm grateful that someone is treating me with basic decency?"

"No, I-"

"Because I'm not some wounded girl. I'm not thanking you for showing me a sliver of kindness." Ruby's voice quivered. "I'm thanking you for understanding my needs. And I'm thanking you for believing I could handle this, despite everything. So just accept my damn thanks and don't treat me like I'm broken."

"You're right. I'm sorry." Yvonne shook her head. "I don't think you're broken. I just don't want you to think that this was performing some selfless act. I enjoyed it too. Your gratitude is misplaced."

Ruby let out an exasperated sigh. "That's so typical of you. You're always doing this."

"Doing this? Doing what?"

"Pretending you don't have a heart."

Yvonne frowned. "I don't do that."

"Yes, you do. Whenever you do something nice for me, or for anyone else, you're always so dismissive. You pretend that it doesn't mean anything, that all your motivations are selfish."

"Because they usually are."

"What about this whole marriage thing?" Ruby said. "You married a stranger to help someone else, right? Nita?"

"It wasn't just for Nita. I have other reasons for wanting that money. I didn't want my brother to get it. And I need it to recoup my investments."

"Sure, you say that. But if it wasn't for Nita, would you have still married me?"

Yvonne hesitated. Did she even know the answer to that?

Ruby threw her hands up. "See, this is what I mean! You act like you're this awful, cold-hearted person when you're not. You act like you don't care about anyone when you do. You're always pushing everyone away so that you'll end up all alone because that's what you think you want, when really you're just trying to protect yourself."

Yvonne raised an eyebrow. "When we met, you said you were a therapist. Is that what this is?"

"You're avoiding the question. I'm not wrong, am I? You're afraid of people hurting you, rejecting you."

Yvonne crossed her arms. "What do you want me to say, Ruby? That I'm all hung up on the fact that I spent most of my life being shoved aside, being resented just for existing?"

"It wouldn't be surprising if you were."

"I'm not. I don't think about any of that."

"Maybe you don't think about it," Ruby said. "But you feel it. I know you do."

Yvonne opened her mouth to protest, but she found she couldn't. It was true. Yvonne did feel it. She'd never stopped feeling it. And she felt it more than ever now that Ruby had come along and made Yvonne want to open up to her.

But how could Yvonne open up to anyone? Every time in her life, when she'd sought love and acceptance, she'd been abandoned, rejected, hurt. Her mother had left her alone in the world before she was old enough to find her own way. Her father, the one man who was supposed to love her, had seen her as a nuisance, something he wished he could get rid of. Her stepmother, her brother, had treated her with such contempt, had made her feel alone and unwanted like she wasn't deserving of her father's love, or anyone else's.

"Believe me, I understand how hard it is to trust after you've been hurt. But if you give people a chance, you'll see that it's worth it." Ruby placed her hand on Yvonne's arm. "You need to stop pushing everyone away."

Yvonne sighed. "It's hard to break old habits. I've become so accustomed to living this way."

"Lucky for you, I'm one person you can't push away. I'm not going anywhere. We signed a contract. Two, in fact. And we took a vow. You're stuck with me." Ruby planted a gentle kiss on Yvonne's cheek. "Now lie back down. I need to finish that massage."

Yvonne felt a spike of irritation at Ruby's bossiness. Nevertheless, she lay down again, closed her eyes and rested her head in her arms once more.

As Yvonne surrendered to the other woman's touch, Ruby's words played in her mind. *I'm not going anywhere.* That wasn't quite true. Their arrangement had an expiration date. When the year was over, Ruby would be gone.

Could Yvonne really let Ruby walk out of her life?

CHAPTER 23

Yvonne sat at her desk in the Mistress Media offices, replying to the last of her emails. It was evening, and she was eager to head home to her apartment. Ruby had messaged her earlier with a photo of a dozen meticulously decorated cupcakes she'd made, along with a promise to save the best of the batch for her Mistress. While Yvonne didn't care for baked goods, Ruby's enthusiasm for them made Yvonne smile.

She sighed. The three-month mark was fast approaching. Soon, Yvonne would have her hands on half of her inheritance. It would be enough to help Nita, enough to recoup her own investments. All her problems would be solved.

And Ruby would have half her money too.

There was a knock on Yvonne's office door. She looked up to find Madison entering the room, her coat and briefcase slung over her arm.

"Still here?" Madison asked. "I thought your days of staying late at the office were in the past."

"They are," Yvonne said. "I'm finishing up now."

"I'm about to head out too. Just waiting for Blair to wrap things up. We have a dinner date." Madison took a seat in the chair in front of Yvonne's desk. "While I wait, there are some matters I need to discuss with you, I'll need you to take care of while we're on the honeymoon."

Madison's honeymoon was just over a week away. While she was gone, Yvonne would have to take over the running of Mistress Media. It would mostly be business as usual for Yvonne, but Madison insisted on reminding her of every little task and meeting Yvonne would have to attend to in her place.

As Madison continued, Yvonne's mind drifted back to Ruby. Ruby hadn't mentioned anything about ending their arrangement at three months. She'd implied she was sticking the entire year through. But after the year was over, what would happen to the two of them?

What did Yvonne want to happen?

"Can you take care of it?" Madison said.

Yvonne blinked. "Yes. Leave it to me." She had no idea what Madison had said, but as always, Madison would email her about it later.

Madison looked at her, frowning. "Okay, what's going on?"

"Nothing. Everything is fine."

Madison put her coat and bag down. "Don't tell me. It's about Ruby."

"Is it really that obvious?"

"I've never seen anyone get under your skin as much as her. It's the only explanation. So, what's the problem? The honeymoon period is finally over?"

"No, everything between us is great. That's the thing." Yvonne paused. "I'm becoming attached to her."

"Attached?" Madison raised an eyebrow. "Yvonne, Ruby isn't a puppy. And the fact that you feel something toward her isn't a bad thing."

"It complicates things. This arrangement of ours, it was never supposed to be anything more than temporary."

"But you want it to be more?"

Yvonne shook her head. "I don't know. Perhaps I should ask Ruby what she wants."

"Isn't it obvious what Ruby wants? She's clearly head over heels for you."

Yvonne scoffed. "I don't know what you mean."

Madison stared at her, incredulous. "You can't be serious. You really don't see it?"

"See what? Perhaps there's some attraction there, but I imagine it has something to do with the fact that I know how to handle a whip."

Madison shook her head. "It's so much more than that. The night you brought her to Lilith's Den, it was obvious to me that the two of you were faking it. But when I saw you with Ruby at my wedding, both of you were completely different people. I've long suspected you have feelings for her, but I didn't know Ruby was into you too until then. All the signs were there. The way she was hanging off your arm like she never wanted to let go. The way she spoke about you-"

Yvonne held up her hand. "That was acting, on both our ends. It's no surprise that Ruby is good at it. It's her job, to become whoever her client needs her to be. It's not real."

"Yvonne, that *wasn't* acting. The way Ruby looks at you,

it's like you're her everything. She's completely and utterly enamored with you. You'd have to be blind not to see it." Madison folded her arms across her chest. "You're not blind, Yvonne. You're making excuses. Why are you so afraid of telling her how you feel? Why are you so afraid of admitting to yourself how you feel?"

Yvonne frowned. "I'm not-"

There was a knock on the door. Through the glass, Blair waved at Madison, then entered the room.

She looked from Madison to Yvonne. "I interrupted something, didn't I? I can wait outside."

"It's fine," Yvonne said. "You're not interrupting."

Blair addressed Madison. "I'm ready when you are."

"Let's get going." Madison rose from her chair. "We don't want to be late for dinner."

"Speaking of which, when are you and Ruby going to come over for dinner?" Blair said. "I had a great time talking to her at the wedding. She's lovely."

"She is, isn't she?" Madison said. "I agree, you simply must bring her around for dinner one of these days."

Yvonne shot Madison a pointed look. "I'll talk to Ruby about it."

"Good." Madison gave Yvonne a knowing smile, then turned to Blair. "Let's go."

They left the room, Blair on Madison's arm. Even Yvonne had to admit the two of them were ridiculously sweet together. They were definitely still deep in the honeymoon period.

She shut her laptop, packed up her desk and left the building. It was still rush hour, so she didn't bother calling a cab, instead opting to walk the few blocks home. She had plenty of thinking to do. For starters, she needed to ask someone to come with her and Ruby to the upcoming meeting with the executor of her father's estate to act as their witness.

Who would she choose? Yvonne had very few close friends. Madison was out of the question because she knew the truth about Yvonne and Ruby's marriage. Plus, she was leaving for her honeymoon the same day. One of the others, perhaps? She didn't know Lydia well enough to feel comfortable asking her. That left Gabrielle and Amber. Although Gabrielle would gladly help Yvonne out, her blunt manner meant there was a chance she'd unknowingly let something slip that would give Yvonne and Ruby away. Amber was far more reliable, and her status as an heiress to a reputable family gave her a certain authority.

Yvonne reached her apartment and got into the elevator, making a mental note to talk to Amber as she did. She was sure Amber would agree to help them out. Amber had no reason not to believe Yvonne and Ruby were a real couple. They had done an excellent job of convincing everyone of that over the past few months.

Was there a reason for that? Was Madison right? Was Ruby head over heels for Yvonne?

Was Yvonne head over heels for Ruby too?

She made her way to her front door. Ruby was inside waiting for her, cupcakes and all. For once, Yvonne didn't feel like she was alone. She had Ruby. Ruby was hers.

Could Ruby be hers for good? Was that what Yvonne wanted?

Yvonne wasn't the type to be plagued with insecurities. She rarely felt uncertain about anything. So why was she so uncertain about this? Was she simply making excuses? Was Yvonne afraid of her feelings for Ruby, afraid of getting hurt?

Yvonne took a moment to collect herself, then slid her key into the lock. But when she turned it, it didn't make its usual click.

The door was unlocked.

Yvonne frowned. Perhaps Ruby simply had forgotten to lock the door after returning home.

She opened the door and entered her apartment. "Ruby?"

Ruby didn't respond, but Yvonne could hear voices coming from the direction of the bedrooms. As she approached, she heard Ruby speaking in a raised, shrill tone.

"Give it back!"

Yvonne's pulse sped up. She raced to Ruby's room, her heart in her throat.

When she reached the doorway, she froze. Ruby was cowering by her dresser, her arms held close, hugging herself.

Standing before her was Yvonne's brother.

"Get away from her," Yvonne said. "*Now.*"

Nicholas turned toward Yvonne, his face twisting into a smile. "Yvonne. You're home." He stepped away from Ruby.

Ruby's eyes widened. "Yvonne, I'm sorry!"

"What the hell are you doing here?" Yvonne snapped.

"I came to see you," Nicholas replied. "I wanted to discuss this inheritance issue of yours, but since you weren't home, I decided I'd come in and wait."

"He just burst in here," Ruby said. "I couldn't stop him."

Yvonne's stomach turned to ice. "If you laid a hand on Ruby-"

"I didn't touch her," Nicholas said. "She let me in, so I thought I'd take the opportunity to have a look around. You've lived here for years, but you haven't invited me over before. I've never seen the place."

Yvonne looked at Ruby. "Are you all right? Did he hurt you?"

"No, I'm fine." Ruby's voice trembled. "I'm so sorry, I tried to stop him."

Yvonne examined her. Ruby seemed unharmed, but why did she keep apologizing? "What are you talking about? What did he do?"

Ruby looked at Nicholas. Yvonne followed the path of her eyes. Nicholas was holding a document in his hands. Yvonne's heart plummeted from her chest.

The contract.

Before Nicholas could react, Yvonne snatched it out of his hand.

Nicholas smirked. "It's too late for that. I've already seen it. I've read it. I know the truth about your arrangement." He crossed his arms. "When I started looking around, all I was hoping to find was something that showed you weren't really a couple. Separate bedrooms, maybe. But this? This is a jackpot."

"It's just a prenup," Yvonne said.

"A very unconventional one. And it's dated after you got married."

"I told you, the wedding was a spur of the moment thing."

"Because it's a lie!" He waved his hands around him. "All

of this, it's a big lie. You entered into a fraudulent marriage, and you were stupid enough to put the terms down in a contract. That's so like you. Such a control freak." He looked at Ruby, licking his lips. "The other contract I found just proves how much of a freak you are."

Yvonne looked down at the papers in her hands. Sure enough, underneath the marriage contract was the other contract Yvonne and Ruby had signed.

It was enough to bring Yvonne to her senses. Why was she standing here, arguing with Nicholas? He'd invaded their home, invaded her and Ruby's privacy.

He had crossed a line.

Anger boiled up inside her. "Get out. Get out of this room. Get out of my apartment. Get out before I call the police and have you arrested for assault."

"Happily," Nicholas said. "After all, I have all the evidence I need. And I'm going to tell the world the truth. There's no way you're going to get your hands on that inheritance now."

"Get. Out."

"Settle down." Nicholas held up his hands defensively. "I'm leaving." Giving Ruby one last glare, he left the room.

Yvonne followed Nicholas out into the hall and marched him to the door. She opened it wide, shoving him through it.

"One last thing, Nicholas," she said. "Don't you ever, *ever* come near me or Ruby again."

Before he could react, Yvonne slammed the door in his face.

Yvonne leaned back against the door and closed her eyes, taking a deep breath, trying to stifle the fury burning inside her. Nicholas had come to her home, had intruded on her space. He'd violated her privacy, violated *Ruby's* space and privacy.

And now, he was going to expose them.

"Fuck!" She clenched her fists. Everything was falling apart.

Yvonne's phone pinged inside her purse, which she'd dropped near the door on the way in. She took her phone out and checked it, a reflex from years of fielding important after-hours work emails. But it wasn't work. The notification was a message from her brother containing a link.

Yvonne's stomach dropped. She opened the link. What she saw shattered the last vestiges of hope she'd had.

She slid down the door and sank to the floor, burying her head in her arms.

∼

Ruby stared at her bedroom wall, replaying the events of the last hour over and over in her head. When Nicholas had turned up at the door and bulldozed his way inside, she'd frozen. Being confronted by a large aggressive man while all alone in her home had sent her mind right back to her past, with her former client, when she'd been powerless and afraid.

By the time she'd come to her senses, it had been too late. She hadn't been able to stop Nicholas from going through the house. She hadn't been able to stop him from finding the contract.

And now, everything was ruined.

Ruby took a few deep breaths, trying to settle the

anxiety simmering within her. She should check on Yvonne. It was the least Ruby could do, considering this was all her fault. How was Yvonne handling everything? Ruby had heard Yvonne's bedroom door slam shut earlier. She didn't know how much time had passed since then. She'd been lost in her own head.

Overcoming her paralysis, Ruby rose from the bed and headed to Yvonne's bedroom. She knocked on the door.

"Yvonne?" There was no response, but Ruby heard footsteps pacing inside. "Yvonne, I'm coming in, okay?"

Yvonne didn't answer her, but the footsteps stopped. Ruby opened the door gingerly. Yvonne was standing in front of the window, staring out into the darkness of the night, her body tense and tight.

"Yvonne?" Ruby stepped inside the room tentatively. "Are you okay?"

Yvonne's shoulders stiffened, but she didn't turn around. "What do you think, Ruby?"

Yvonne's hard tone made Ruby's stomach lurch. "Yvonne, I'm sorry," she blurted out. "I shouldn't have let him in here. I didn't mean to, I just froze, and… I shouldn't have left the contracts just sitting out. But we can fix this, can't we?"

"It's too late," Yvonne said flatly. "Nicholas, he posted photos of the contracts on social media for all to see."

Ruby's heart sank. *"Both* the contracts?"

"Yes, both the contracts. We've been exposed."

Ruby barely cared about the fact that everyone now knew the intimate details of their arrangement. What she cared about was how much this was clearly hurting Yvonne.

Ruby approached her. Her back was still turned, but as

Ruby drew closer, she saw Yvonne's face reflected in the window, warped with despair.

"Yvonne, everything is going to be okay."

Yvonne shook her head. "No, it's not. There's no way I can get my inheritance now. All that money, gone. How am I going to help Nita?" Her voice cracked. "And now everyone knows our marriage is a lie. Do you have any idea how humiliating this is? This farce of a relationship, exposed to the entire world."

Ruby felt a pang in her chest. Pushing it aside, she reached out and touched the other woman's shoulder. "Yvonne-"

Yvonne broke away and began pacing before the window. "This was all for nothing. All the lies, the pretending." She threw her hands up. "Almost three months, wasted on this stupid charade. And now, it's over."

The ache in Ruby's chest turned into a stabbing too painful to ignore. "Is there anything I can do to help?" she asked quietly.

"No." Yvonne's voice was devoid of emotion. "Just leave me be."

"I'm sorry, Yvonne. I'm so sorry."

Ruby turned and fled from the room, her eyes stinging with tears. She returned to her bedroom, shut the door, and collapsed onto the bed, Yvonne's words echoing in her mind. Her chest felt hollow. Sure, Ruby had messed up. Sure, she'd ruined things for Yvonne. But did Yvonne truly believe that this was all for nothing, that these three months had been wasted?

Ruby buried her face in her pillow, trying to smother the hurt inside her. She had no right to be upset. The whole point of their marriage was so that Yvonne could get her inheritance. That was all Yvonne had needed Ruby for. From the very beginning, Yvonne had made it clear that their arrangement was purely business.

To Yvonne, Ruby was just a means to an end.

Ruby sat up and yanked the wedding ring from her finger, tossing it to the floor. To think she'd opened up to Yvonne, sharing all her darkest secrets and desires. To think Ruby had trusted Yvonne. To think Ruby had started to believe that what they had was real.

To think she'd started to wonder whether she was falling in love with Yvonne.

Ruby should have known better. She'd been stupid to let her feelings get caught up in everything between them. Stupid to think their arrangement could have been more. Stupid to give her mind, and body, and everything else to this woman who only wanted her for money and pleasure.

She'd been stupid to agree to this sham of a marriage in the first place.

Ruby got up from the bed. She didn't want to stay here. Yvonne herself had said that it was all over.

Ruby went into her closet, grabbed her suitcase, and started to pack.

CHAPTER 24

Yvonne knocked on Ruby's bedroom door. She needed to apologize for her behavior the night before. She was ashamed of how badly she'd reacted to the situation. Everything had been spiraling out of control, and she'd found herself out of her depth.

It wasn't a feeling she was accustomed to. She'd been terrified. The things she'd said to Ruby, the way she'd treated her, had been callous and unfair. Yvonne had been so consumed by the fact that her inheritance plot was falling apart that she hadn't even considered how Ruby's encounter with Nicholas had affected her.

Yvonne knocked on the door again. "Ruby? Are you in there?"

She waited but didn't get a response. It was morning, so there was a chance Ruby was still asleep, but Yvonne needed to talk to her. She waited a few seconds more, then began knocking more insistently.

Just when Yvonne was about to give up, the door swung open.

Ruby stood before her, her face blank and her blue eyes cold. "What is it?"

"You're awake," Yvonne said. Ruby was already fully dressed. She looked like she'd been awake for a while. "Can I come in?"

Ruby stepped aside for Yvonne to enter the room. Ruby took a seat on the edge of her bed, while Yvonne perched on a nearby armchair, taking a moment to gather her thoughts.

"So?" Ruby said. "What do you want?"

Yvonne's stomach tightened. Clearly, she'd hurt Ruby more than she'd realized. "I want to talk about last night. I need to apologize for how I behaved."

"It's fine."

"No, it's not. I should never have said what I did. I never meant to..." Why did Ruby's room look so bare? Yvonne looked around it.

Sitting in the corner were two fully packed suitcases.

Her heart lurched. "Ruby. You're leaving?"

Ruby gave her a dismissive shrug. "It's over. You said so yourself last night."

"I didn't mean-" Yvonne shook her head. "I didn't mean you should *leave*."

"What's the point in staying?"

"Ruby-"

"What, Yvonne? What is it that you want? Do you even know yourself?" Ruby's voice rose. "It's been like this with you from the start. You say you want one thing, but you behave in the complete opposite way. You push me away, then you tell me I'm precious. You play these games with me while saying they mean nothing. Then yesterday, you said that these three months were a waste, that they were all for nothing? What am I supposed to think? How am I supposed to feel?" She shook her head. "I'm so tired of this. Do you ever mean anything you say? Do you ever stop to think about who you hurt just by being the way you are? Or are you just too stuck in your own head to even care?"

Yvonne flinched. "I-"

"Just tell me what you want, Yvonne! For once, just tell me."

"I don't know!" Yvonne stopped and took a deep breath. "I don't know what I want. I just... I don't want to give up on this yet."

"This? What do you mean by 'this?' Do you mean us, or your plan to get your inheritance?"

Yvonne hesitated, just for a moment. But it was long enough.

Ruby scoffed. "That's what I thought. You know what, that's fine with me. If you still want to try to salvage this stupid inheritance plot, I'll stick around. It's almost three months already, I might as well get something out of it."

"Ruby-"

"Tell me what I need to do, Yvonne. That's all you ever do, isn't it? That's all you want from me, right? You want someone you can tell what to do? What to say? Someone who will crawl for your entertainment? Someone you can *own*?"

Something tore inside Yvonne's chest. "Ruby-"

"Just tell me how we can salvage this so I still get my money."

"Fine." Yvonne gritted her jaw. "I don't have any ideas yet, but I'm working on it. If there's even a small chance we can convince Bill that we're really married, I want to take it.

All I need is for you to come to the meeting with me." She paused. "And even if I don't get the inheritance money, I'll still give you your money. Two and a half million. You held up your end of the bargain after all."

"Fine. I'll come to the meeting. I'll stay until then. At least that way, these three months wouldn't be a complete waste," she muttered.

"Ruby, please."

Ruby crossed her arms. "Are we done? I'd like to be alone."

Yvonne remained seated. She couldn't leave things between them like this. She couldn't let this rift between them grow any bigger.

But the pain in Ruby's eyes as she looked at Yvonne was too much to bear.

"Yes," Yvonne said. "We're done."

She rose from her chair, took one last look at the suitcases in the corner, and left the room.

~

"So," Nita said. "To what do I owe the pleasure of this visit?"

Yvonne blew on her tea. "Do I need an excuse to come see you?"

"No, but you usually have one."

"I just wanted to check on you. See how you're doing."

"I'm doing fine," Nita said. "That check you gave us really helped. It's given us some room to breathe."

"Soon, you'll be able to breathe easy for good. I'm going to get you that money, just like I promised you."

"Yvonne, you don't have to do that."

Yvonne crossed her arms. "We're not having this argument again. The money is coming. I need a little more time, that's all."

Yvonne had no idea how she was going to find the money if she didn't get her inheritance. She also needed to find the money she'd promised Ruby. She could sell off some assets, but she'd lose millions. It would take her years to rebuild.

Yvonne suppressed a sigh. Right now, money wasn't even her biggest problem. She also had to deal with the fallout of her brother exposing her and Ruby. She'd lied to the world, and now everything had come tumbling down in a humiliating way. Yvonne didn't care what most people thought of her, but she'd lied to her friends, and now they were angry with her, rightfully so. She felt awful about it. She'd been lying to herself when she'd said she didn't care about deceiving her friends.

You act like you're this awful, cold-hearted person when you're not.

Ruby had been right. Yvonne pretended she didn't have a heart, but she obviously did, otherwise she wouldn't feel the way she did right now. She'd hurt Ruby badly, and not just last night. Yvonne had been heartless toward her from the start. She'd shut Ruby out, she'd pushed her away time and time again, just like she'd done to everyone else.

But Ruby wasn't like everyone else. She didn't walk away from Yvonne at the bar that night. She didn't walk away every time Yvonne turned her back on her. Ruby kept trying to break down Yvonne's walls, and all because she saw something in Yvonne that made her not want to give up on her.

But Yvonne didn't deserve her.

"Now, what's going on with you?" Nita asked. "How's that wife of yours? You still need to bring her around so I can meet her."

Yvonne's stomach knotted. "That's… not going to happen."

"Why not? Did something happen between the two of you?"

"We-" Yvonne's hands began to tremble. All of a sudden, everything she was feeling became too much. She gripped her teacup tighter. "I messed up, Nita. I messed everything up."

"I'm sure that's not true. Whatever you did, I'm sure Ruby will forgive you for it."

"It wasn't just one thing. This entire time, I treated her badly, I took her for granted. And now, I've really hurt her." Yvonne shook her head. "She didn't deserve any of it."

"Oh, Xiǎo táo." Nita reached across the table and put her hand on Yvonne's. "You really care about her, don't you?"

"More than I've ever cared about anyone."

"Then you have to fight for her."

"No," Yvonne said quietly. "It's too complicated. This arrangement of ours, this farce of a marriage, I should have never let things get this far. I should have never let the lines get so blurred."

The room fell silent. Nita folded her arms on the table before her, her eyes wandering off into the distance.

"There's something I've never told you," she said. "It's about Mark and me. You see, our marriage was an arrangement of sorts too."

Yvonne stared at her. "Really?" That explained why Nita had been so quick to accept Yvonne and Ruby's marriage.

"It's true. We barely knew each other when we got married, and we certainly weren't in love. You never thought it was odd that I got married out of the blue? I suppose you were too young to notice."

Yvonne vaguely remembered Nita getting married when she was around ten years old. Her father had forbidden her from going to the wedding, as it wouldn't have been 'appropriate' due to Nita's status as the help.

Nita leaned back in her chair. "The story isn't the least bit exciting. I was in my late twenties and single as could be. It had my parents worried. They were very traditional. They were concerned that I wouldn't be able to find someone to marry at such an 'old' age. Eventually, they decided to take matters into their own hands and find me a husband, all under the guise of matchmaking."

"And you let them? That doesn't sound like the Nita I know."

"Of course I didn't. I resisted every step of the way. My parents presented me with an endless stream of potential husbands. To my parents' dismay, I turned them all down in the rudest way possible. That was, until Mark."

Nita's eyes grew distant. "He was the son of a family friend. My parents invited him and his parents over for dinner without telling me. I was furious until I saw him. He was one of the most handsome people I'd ever seen. But he soon proved to be arrogant and frustrating."

Hadn't Yvonne felt that way too, when she'd first laid eyes on Ruby? That intense physical attraction, followed immediately by irritation?

"After dinner, our parents sent the two of us out for a walk, alone. We ended up wandering the neighborhood for what seemed like hours, venting to each other about how crazy our parents were when it came to marriage. His were even worse than mine. And on that walk, he proposed that we marry each other just to get them off our backs. Against all my better judgment, I agreed. A couple of months later, we were married.

"We moved in together and basically became roommates, playing the happy couple for our parents. But slowly, the two of us grew closer. Slowly, we went from roommates to something more." Nita smiled. "And here we are, three kids and almost twenty-five years later, still together."

"I had no idea," Yvonne said. "The two of you seem like such a normal married couple."

"That's because we are. Why do you think I've stuck with Mark through everything he's put the family through with this business of his, all the mistakes he's made? It's because I love him. Yvonne, sometimes fate throws people together. But embracing that fate, embracing love? That's a choice only you can make."

Yvonne shook her head. "What's between Ruby and me, it isn't fate, or love. It's just money, and sex, and emotions."

"Do you truly believe that, or are you just telling yourself that because it makes this easier?"

Yvonne didn't answer her.

Nita tilted her head, studying Yvonne. "Why did you marry Ruby in the first place?"

Yvonne frowned. Did she even know the answer herself? While she'd ostensibly gotten married to solve a problem, was that truly the only reason she'd married Ruby? Had there been a part of her that had simply married Ruby because she'd felt that pull, that attraction to her, from the moment their eyes had met in that bar?

Would Yvonne have gone through with the marriage if she hadn't felt anything toward Ruby at all?

She sighed. "It doesn't matter. Everything between us is too messy, too complicated. It was never going to work."

There was no point in fighting it. Ruby's bags were packed. She already had one foot out the door.

It was over.

CHAPTER 25

Yvonne parked her car out the front of Bill Marsden's law offices. She'd come straight from work. Ruby hadn't arrived yet, but she'd promised to show.

Not that it mattered at this point. Yvonne had spent the entire week trying to think of a way to convince Bill to give her the money, but she hadn't come up with anything. She didn't know if the news that her marriage to Ruby was a sham had reached Bill himself, but even if it hadn't, Yvonne didn't have a witness to vouch for them. The meeting was pointless.

She got out of the car. As she spotted Ruby heading in her direction, she felt a tightness in her chest. Over the course of the past week and a half, the two of them had barely spoken to, or even seen each other, despite still living together. The gulf that had formed between them was insurmountable.

Yvonne approached her. "Ready to go in?"

Ruby nodded.

"Ruby, I-"

"Let's just do this."

Yvonne headed into the office, Ruby behind her. After speaking to Bill's secretary, they took a seat in the waiting room. They were early, so they sat in silence while they waited. Ruby wouldn't even look at Yvonne.

After a few minutes, the door to the waiting room swung open. In walked Madison, dressed casually and looking hurried.

She spotted Yvonne. "Good, you're here."

Yvonne frowned. "What are you doing here?" Madison was due to leave for her honeymoon later in the evening. "Shouldn't you be at the airport? Is there a problem?"

"No, everything is fine. We rescheduled our flight for tomorrow morning."

"Why? What's going on?"

"I'm here to be your witness."

Yvonne blinked. "What are you talking about?" She lowered her voice. "I'm not going to ask you to lie for me."

"I don't intend to."

"I don't understand-"

The door to Bill's office opened. An older man wearing a pair of reading glasses stepped out into the waiting room.

"Yvonne, are you ready?" Bill said.

Yvonne looked at Madison, who nodded. She looked at Ruby, who would barely meet her eye. Yvonne wasn't ready at all.

But there was no point in delaying the inevitable.

"We're ready," Yvonne said.

She stood up and followed Bill into his office, Ruby and Madison behind her.

"Hello, Yvonne."

A chill went down Yvonne's spine. She turned to see Nicholas leaning casually against the wall, a dark look on his face.

"Nicholas," Yvonne hissed. "What the hell are you doing here? Didn't I tell you to stay away from me and Ruby?"

"What do you think? I was just telling Bill all about your little marriage arrangement." Nicholas crossed his arms. "Did you think I was going to let you get away with this? Did you think I was going to let some hooker get her paws on Father's money?"

Yvonne's hands curled into fists. "You-"

Bill cleared his throat. "Now, let's all have a seat and calm down. Everyone will get a chance to speak."

Anger simmering inside her, Yvonne took a seat in front of Bill's desk alongside Ruby and Madison. Nicholas remained standing, his expression smug. It was taking all Yvonne's effort to remain civil.

"Now," Bill addressed Ruby. "You must be Yvonne's wife. Ruth Scott, is it?"

Ruby nodded.

He turned to Madison. "And I take it this is your witness?"

"Yes." Madison held out her hand and gave Bill's a firm shake. "Madison Sloane."

"Sloane? Ah, I believe I went to school with your father. How is he?"

"Can we get on with this, please?" Yvonne didn't want to remain in the same room as her brother any longer than necessary.

"Yes, of course." Bill opened a folder on his desk. "Now Yvonne. To begin with, I've heard some troubling things from your brother. He tells me that you and Ruth entered into a fraudulent marriage in order to gain access to your inheritance, among other things. These are some serious accusations. However, considering your brother has something to gain from you not receiving your inheritance, it's important that I hear your side of the story."

Nicholas spoke up from the corner. "Her side of the story? Isn't it obvious? This whole marriage of theirs is a scam. I've shown you the evidence."

Bill ignored him. "I'm giving you the chance to show that these accusations are false. Do you have anything to say, Yvonne? Are the accusations true? Is your marriage fraudulent?"

Yvonne hesitated. She couldn't lie. Not anymore. "I-"

"No," Madison interrupted. "It's not."

Yvonne turned to stare at her. What the hell was Madison doing?

"You'll have to forgive the interruption, but there's something that needs to be said. Yvonne and Ruby's relationship isn't fraudulent. And I can attest to that."

Bill pushed his glasses up his nose. "Go on."

"You see, Yvonne is like a sister to me," Madison said. "I've known her since we were teenagers. That's why I'm confident in saying that her relationship with Ruby is genuine." She gestured toward Ruby. "I don't know Ruby well, but I've seen her and Yvonne together. I've seen how happy they make each other. I've seen how much Yvonne's relationship with Ruby has changed her, for the better."

Madison looked at Yvonne. "I've seen the way Ruby looks at her. I've seen the way Yvonne looks at Ruby. It's obvious that they're wildly, madly in love."

Something knotted inside Yvonne's stomach. She knew what Madison was doing. She knew what Madison was trying to tell her.

She knew what she had to do.

Bill nodded in Madison's direction. "That was a very moving speech, Madison." He looked at Yvonne. "Yvonne? Do you have anything to say?"

Yvonne steeled herself. She wasn't going to let this opportunity slip away.

"Yes, I do," she said. "What Madison said is true. My relationship with Ruby is real."

Beside her, Ruby shifted in her seat, but she said nothing.

Nicholas scoffed. "This is ridiculous. The two of you aren't in love. Ruby's an escort. This is all fake!"

"Nicholas," Bill warned. "Let Yvonne-"

"Why are you even entertaining this?" Nicholas threw up his hands. "You've seen the evidence for yourself. I've shown you the contract."

"The contract you broke into my apartment to steal?" Yvonne folded her arms across her chest. "This evidence of yours was obtained illegally. You're lucky I didn't have you arrested."

"That doesn't matter," Nicholas said. "This isn't a court. How I got the evidence doesn't make it invalid."

"That's true. But the contract you found isn't evidence of anything. So Ruby and I have a document outlining the financial side of our marriage. It isn't the only contract we have. You've seen it for yourself, haven't you? The other contract, outlining the more intimate details of our relationship? It's no different. I simply like to set clear boundaries in all aspects of my marriage."

"This is crazy!" Nicholas turned to Bill, eyes wide and nostrils flaring. "Can't you see that this is just one big scheme? You can't be stupid enough to believe any of this."

"That's enough, Nicholas," Bill said sharply. "You've had your chance to speak, and insulting my intelligence isn't going to help your case. Your father raised you better than this. Now shut up or leave my office."

Nicholas scowled, but didn't say anything further.

Bill's calm demeanor returned. "Yvonne, I'll ask you again. Are Nicholas's accusations true?"

"You want the truth?" Yvonne stood up. "The truth is, everything my brother said is true. And so is everything Madison said."

Silence filled the room. For what had to be the first time in more than a week, Ruby looked Yvonne in the eyes, her face a mix of surprise and confusion.

"Ruby is an escort," Yvonne said. "We got married in Vegas. We barely knew each other when we did it, and we were drunk. It was entirely spontaneous and ill thought out, and we only decided to stay married because of the money." She turned to Ruby. "But in the months since then, I've fallen for Ruby completely."

Ruby's mouth fell open slightly. Yvonne didn't stop to think about whether Ruby's shock was the good kind. She needed to power through this.

"Ruby, these past months—all the moments we've shared in that time—they've made me feel more than I've felt in years. You made me feel things I didn't know I could even feel, made me want things I never, ever thought I'd want.

You got me to open up my heart in a way I've always been so afraid to do."

Yvonne got down on her knees. "You make me happier than I ever thought I could be. I can't even begin to tell you how much you mean to me. And when I look at you, I don't see the stranger I met in a bar in Vegas. I see an incredible woman, so vibrant, so kind-hearted, so beautiful. And I've been so lucky to share my life and my heart with that woman."

Yvonne looked into Ruby's eyes. They shimmered with light.

"And through all that, I treated you badly," Yvonne said. "I've been so scared of letting you in that I pushed you away, I shut you out, I hurt you. I'm sorry. You didn't deserve any of it. I don't deserve you." Yvonne bowed her head. "But if you can find it in your heart to forgive me, I'll make up for it every single day. I'll show you how I feel about you every single day."

She took Ruby's hand. "Our marriage, it may have been an arrangement, but what I feel for you is real. I love you, Ruby. And in the face of that, all of this—the inheritance, the money—none of it matters. You've given me something priceless. So I don't care if our marriage is deemed real or not. I don't care if I get my inheritance, as long as I have you."

Ruby's hand trembled in hers. "Yvonne..."

Ruby reached out and put a hand on Yvonne's cheek, tilting Yvonne's face up to gaze into her eyes.

"I... I love you too."

Yvonne's heart surged. She stood up, swept Ruby into her arms and kissed her urgently. She never wanted to let

Ruby go.

Bill cleared his throat loudly. "All right. I've heard enough."

Yvonne broke away from Ruby and sat back down. Her hand still held Ruby's, and the warmth in her chest remained. She didn't care about the money anymore. She'd find a way to help Nita. As long as she had Ruby, everything would be all right.

Bill looked at them both. "I don't know exactly what's going on here, but it's impossible to deny that this relationship of yours is genuine. Your brother's protests aside, you have a witness, a reliable, reputable member of the community who has known you your whole life. You certainly appear to be in love. In my eyes, you've met all the conditions to be given your inheritance. I see no reason to withhold the money from you."

Ruby squeezed Yvonne's hand and smiled at her. This was it. The money was theirs.

"What?" Nicholas sputtered, his face turning red. "No. This isn't fair! That money is mine. Can't you see that this is all a scam?"

"Nicholas," Bill began.

Yvonne held up her hand. "I'll handle this." She stood up and walked over to Nicholas, putting her hand on his arm. "You lost, Nicholas. Accept it gracefully. Leave."

Nicholas's mouth gaped open and shut, his face getting even redder.

"Before you go." Yvonne gave him a withering glare, her grip on his arm tightening just enough for him to feel it. "If you ever hurt Ruby again. If you so much as go near Ruby again, I will *end you*."

For a moment, Nicholas stood there, staring back at Yvonne. Then, without a word, he pulled himself from her grip and stormed out of the room. With luck, this would be the last time Yvonne ever saw Nicholas. Now that she had her inheritance, she didn't need to go to those family dinners anymore. She had no reason to keep toxic people like Nicholas and her stepmother in her life any longer.

Bill shut the file on his desk. "That certainly was dramatic." He addressed Yvonne. "As per the terms of the inheritance, I'll transfer half the funds to you now and the rest in nine months. Provided you're still married, that is."

"We will be," Ruby said.

"Then it's settled. The money will be in your account by this evening. And Yvonne?"

"Yes?" Yvonne said.

"I knew your mother, back before you were born. I have no doubt she'd be proud of the woman you've become."

∼

Ruby and Yvonne left Bill's office. Ruby's head was spinning. She still couldn't believe everything that had just happened.

She turned to her wife. "Yvonne."

Yvonne took her hand. "Ruby."

Beside them, Madison cleared her throat. "I should get going. I'll leave you two to it."

Yvonne grabbed Madison's arm. "Wait. I need to thank you for what you did in there. For being our witness. For showing me how much of a fool I've been."

"That's what friends are for. Besides, I couldn't just stand by and watch everything fall apart between the two of you. I had to give you a push." Madison smiled. "Now, if the two of you will excuse me, I'm going to go tell Blair how everything went."

"You told her the truth about us?" Yvonne asked.

"I kept it a secret at first, but you know how she is. It's impossible to keep anything from her."

Yvonne frowned. "If Blair knew about everything, why did she keep trying to invite us to dinner?"

"What can I say? She thought the two of you make a good couple."

Yvonne shook her head. "Just go. And enjoy your honeymoon."

"We will." Madison pulled them both in for a hug before walking off.

"Now," Yvonne took Ruby's hand again. "Where were we?"

"I just can't believe it," Ruby said. "Everything worked out in the end. You got the money. You can help Nita now."

"You're right. The money is ours. You'll get your share, too. But everything I said in there is true. None of that matters to me, not anymore. This marriage of ours was never real. It was never meant to last. But I don't ever want it to end. I want to spend my life with you. And I promise I'll never play games with your heart again."

Ruby's heart swelled. "I know. I believe you. I trust you. And I'm sorry, too. I'm sorry for the horrible things I said to you. I was so cruel. None of it was true." She locked eyes with Yvonne. "I meant what I said in there too. I love you, Yvonne."

"I love you too."

Yvonne leaned in to kiss her. Ruby deepened the kiss, warmth rising within her. God, how she'd missed her Mistress's lips. Not to mention all the other parts of her.

Sensing the longing in Ruby's kiss, Yvonne broke away. "Why don't we go home and celebrate?"

Ruby smiled. "What did you have in mind?"

"Let's just say, I'm not planning to make you a candlelit dinner." Yvonne leaned in close, her words tickling Ruby's ear. "Although I can't guarantee there won't be kitchen utensils involved."

Ruby's cheeks flushed. "All right. Let's go home."

CHAPTER 26

As soon as they stepped through the front door of the apartment, Yvonne pushed Ruby up against the wall, pressing her lips to Ruby's. Ruby's soft gasp, the way her body crumbled against Yvonne's, sent an invigorating shiver through her. Yvonne had to have Ruby, now. She'd already told Ruby how she felt about her.

Now, she was going to show her.

Their lips still locked, Yvonne dragged Ruby through the apartment in a frenzy of passion, heedless of the furniture and doorways they were bumping into. When they reached the door to the playroom, Yvonne pushed Ruby away, eliciting a whimpered protest.

"Wait here," Yvonne said.

Ruby pouted but obeyed. Yvonne opened the door and entered the room, shutting it behind her. She wanted a moment to prepare herself. More importantly, she wanted to make Ruby wait.

It always made the pleasure so much sweeter.

Yvonne pulled her hair out of the bun she'd put it up in

for work, shaking it out so it settled over her shoulders. She removed her coat, slipped out of her heels, and peeled down her pantyhose, taking her panties off in the process. She pushed them under the armchair behind her and sat down in it before sliding her heels back on.

Yvonne placed her arms on the armrests and crossed her legs. "You can open the door now," she called.

Ruby opened the door tentatively and peered inside. Spotting Yvonne in the chair, a smile crossed her lips. She stepped into the room.

Yvonne gave Ruby a look that stopped her in her tracks. "I didn't say to come in."

Ruby took a step back, her head lowered. However, she couldn't help but peer up at Yvonne from under her eyelashes.

Yvonne leaned back in her chair. "Strip."

A visible flush crept up Ruby's cheeks. Slowly, she reached for her waistband, pulling her blouse free, and drawing it over her head. She slipped out of her skirt with a shimmy of her hips, an obvious attempt to tease Yvonne. Yvonne wasn't going to let it slide. She would deal with her submissive's attempt at seduction later.

As Ruby reached around her back to remove her bra, Yvonne issued another command.

"Stop."

Ruby froze again.

"Get on your hands and knees."

Yvonne watched understanding slowly dawn on Ruby's face, relishing it. Ruby got down on her knees, then her hands.

"Now," Yvonne said. "Come to your Mistress."

Silence fell over the room. Slowly, Ruby crawled across the floor toward Yvonne. Deep in Yvonne's core, heat flickered and flared. She shifted in her seat, trying to smother it, but by the time Ruby reached her, Yvonne's desire had only grown.

Yvonne looked down at Ruby. The other woman's long, straight locks hung over her face like a golden veil. Yvonne's breath deepened. Ruby before her, at her feet, worshipping her—it made her heart surge just as much as it filled her with need.

"My precious Ruby." Yvonne reached down, brushed Ruby's hair out of her face, and tipped her chin up. Her eyes brimmed with lust. Yvonne was certain her own eyes matched Ruby's.

Yvonne uncrossed her legs, parting them just a few inches. Ruby's eyes zeroed in between them, her lips parting slightly.

"Do you want to serve me?" Yvonne asked.

"Yes, Mistress," Ruby whispered.

Yvonne slid forward in the chair, letting her skirt ride up, parting her legs further.

"Then serve me."

Looking up at her expectantly, Ruby reached up to brace herself on Yvonne's knees, only to stop and draw her hand back. Instead, Ruby closed her eyes and nudged the inside of Yvonne's knee with her cheek, pushing it along Yvonne's inner thigh.

Yvonne blew out a long, slow breath. She wanted to savor this slowly. She slid forward further, pushing into Ruby's mouth. Ruby's tongue settled against Yvonne's folds, licking and stroking, swirling and flicking in the most heavenly way.

A tremor went through Yvonne's body. "God, yes." She closed her eyes and gripped the armrests tighter, resisting the urge to bring her hands down to Ruby's head to guide her. Ruby knew what her Mistress wanted, what she needed. With Ruby, Yvonne didn't need to be in control all the time. She could simply let go and allow Ruby to serve her.

Besides, Yvonne fully intended to take back control. Just as soon as she'd finished letting Ruby lavish her with pleasure.

She tipped her head over the back of the chair, a low sigh falling from her. Ruby continued, her tongue circling Yvonne's clit more fervently. A moan escaped Yvonne's lips. She was so close!

"Oh, Ruby-"

Yvonne rose up against Ruby in a divine climax that sent waves of pleasure rolling through her. She sank into them, letting the world around her fall away until there was nothing left but herself, and Ruby, and the passion that bound them together.

When the haze of her orgasm cleared, Yvonne found Ruby kneeling before her, her hands folded in her lap, waiting eagerly.

Yvonne reached down toward her. "You have served your Mistress well." She drew her thumb along Ruby's lower lip. It was slick with Yvonne's juices. "And yet, I find myself unsatisfied."

Ruby looked back at her, the anticipation in her eyes mixing with confusion.

But Yvonne didn't toy with her for too long. "I want to have a little more fun. How would you like to be my plaything for the rest of the night?"

Ruby smiled. "Yes, Mistress. I'm all yours."

Yvonne rose from her chair and walked over to the bed, beckoning Ruby to follow. Ruby crawled after her. Yvonne suppressed a smile. She hadn't even asked, yet Ruby had remained on her hands and knees.

Yvonne reached for the hem of her dress and pulled it over her head, letting it fall to the floor beside Ruby. She removed her bra, adding it to the dress.

"You may rise," she said.

Ruby stood up. Her gaze wandered over Yvonne's nude body greedily. But Yvonne only gave Ruby a few moments to admire her before grabbing her shoulders and pushing her onto the bed.

Ruby stared back up at Yvonne. The surprise in her eyes quickly transformed into desire.

Yvonne climbed onto the bed and took Ruby's shoulders, turning Ruby onto her stomach. She straddled Ruby's body, facing her feet, and pinned Ruby's arms against her sides with her knees.

Ruby wriggled underneath her, purring with delight. Yvonne was starting to enjoy this brand of roughness Ruby loved. It was satisfying, watching Ruby pant and writhe, getting more and more worked up as she did.

With Ruby still squirming underneath her, Yvonne reached into the drawer beside the bed and pulled out a pair of handcuffs. Ruby's eyes grew wide. Yvonne took Ruby's wrists and drew them together at the small of Ruby's back, fastening the handcuffs around Ruby's wrists. Ruby tugged at them, wriggling even harder.

Yvonne delivered a sharp slap to Ruby's ass cheek, then two more for good measure. "Stop it."

Ruby sucked in a breath and stopped moving. Yvonne skimmed her fingertips down one side of Ruby's back, all the way to her ass. She drew it along the curve at the base of Ruby's ass cheek, letting a finger slide between Ruby's thighs.

"You're practically dripping," Yvonne said. "I could make you come in seconds if I wanted to." She pressed Ruby's wet panties into her slit, drawing a shiver from her. "But I'm only getting started."

Yvonne got up from the bed, went over to the dresser and selected one of her riding crops, a shorter one with a narrow leather tip. She returned to the bed to find that Ruby had barely moved, not even to look at what Yvonne was doing. She pushed Ruby's cuffed hands higher up her back, then grabbed the waistband of Ruby's panties, yanking them down her legs.

"I should punish you for defying me with all that teasing, that wriggling." Yvonne drew the riding crop up the back of Ruby's thigh. "Do you need to be punished, Ruby?"

Ruby let out a breath. "Yes, Mistress. *Please*."

Yvonne let out a sharp breath. Ruby was actually begging for her Mistress's riding crop? Yvonne was long past the point of needing confirmation that the two of them were a perfect match, but this showed how right she was.

Gathering herself, she raised the riding crop and brought it down on Ruby's ass cheek, just a few testing taps at first. After each one, Ruby arched up, her body begging for more. Yvonne flicked the crop against her with even more force, eliciting short, soft gasps from her. And when Yvonne struck her even harder, Ruby began to purr again.

"You're a glutton for punishment, aren't you?" Yvonne traced the riding crop around the pink patches it had left on Ruby's ass cheeks. "Fortunately for you, I could do this all night."

Yvonne brought the riding crop down, over and over, each strike punctuated by one of Ruby's delightful squeals. Her whole ass was turning a vivid shade of scarlet, and her nether lips glistened with her arousal.

As Ruby's moans deepened, Yvonne decided it was time to replace pain with pleasure. She let the riding crop wander between Ruby's ass cheeks and down between her lower lips. "You're just about ready to come, aren't you?"

Ruby's response was a drunken murmur. That was enough confirmation for Yvonne. Yvonne tossed the riding crop aside, replacing it between Ruby's legs with her fingers. She slid them over Ruby's slick folds, drawing a groan from her. Yvonne glided her fingers down to Ruby's hard, pebbled nub, circling it gently.

Ruby's ass rose into the air as she pushed back against Yvonne greedily. Yvonne eased off a little, prompting a whine from Ruby, but she stopped trying to rush her Mistress.

After teasing Ruby's clit for a while longer, Yvonne ran her finger down to the other woman's entrance. Ruby moaned, her hands moving higher up her back as she pulled at the handcuffs, her fingers forming fists.

Grabbing onto Ruby's hip, Yvonne slid her fingers inside Ruby's warm heat, filling her slowly. Yvonne was gentle at first, delving into Ruby deeply and deliberately, curling against that spot inside that made her shudder and hitch. But as Ruby's breaths grew heavier, Yvonne picked up the pace, fucking Ruby harder and deeper.

"Mistress," Ruby whispered. "Yes. Yes…"

Yvonne kept her on edge, watching Ruby grow increasingly frantic. Her cuffed hands grasped at the air behind her back and her thighs quivered and shook. As wordless pleas began to spill from Ruby's lips, Yvonne decided to give her the sweet release she was begging for.

Yvonne raised her free hand above Ruby's ass cheeks. All it took were a few short, sharp spanks with her palm, and Ruby cried out, her body trembling as an orgasm took her. Yvonne continued inside her, feeling the other woman's walls gripping her, until at last, Ruby fell silent and still.

Yvonne freed Ruby from the handcuffs and drew her into her arms, assailing her with a hot, hard kiss. Ruby melted into her, her lips soft and needy, her hands clinging limply at Yvonne's waist and shoulders.

After a moment, Ruby pulled back. "I don't want to stop," she murmured. "But I need to catch my breath before I pass out."

Yvonne chuckled. "All right. Come here."

Yvonne gathered Ruby into her arms again and settled back against the pillows. Ruby seemed a world away, and Yvonne was right there with her. The high she got from holding Ruby close, feeling the contentment radiating from her, was far better than the high she got from Ruby's submission.

Her wife's happiness, her pleasure, was far more satisfying than anything else in the world.

EPILOGUE

Ruby watched trees whiz by, the cool breeze whipping around her as the convertible sped down the road, the scent of the sea filling the air. She and Yvonne had been driving for what felt like hours, the city long behind them.

She looked over to Yvonne in the driver's seat. "Are you going to tell me where we're going?"

Yvonne smiled, but she didn't take her eyes off the road. "We're almost there."

Ruby sat back and crossed her arms. What was Yvonne's surprise? Yvonne had a good reason to do something grand. It had been a year since that night they'd gotten married in Vegas. Ruby had been counting down the days. She was feeling anxious about it, but not in a bad way. There was no question of whether she and Yvonne would remain together, but without the marriage agreement binding them, their relationship would enter uncharted territory. Ruby was uncertain of what the future held for them.

But she was certain of how she felt about her wife.

Yvonne pulled the car into a long, winding driveway. The salty ocean scent grew stronger, the melodic chirping of seagulls filling the air. Soon, a house came into view, an enormous sprawling mansion, old, but well kept.

Yvonne parked the car outside the house and turned off the engine. "We're here. Let's go take a look."

Ruby got out of the car and stared up at the house. "Where is here, exactly? What is this place?"

"This is our house," Yvonne said. "Our vacation home, for when we want to escape it all, to get away from all the noise of the city."

Ruby turned to Yvonne, her eyes widening. "You bought this?"

"Consider it an anniversary present."

"But where did you find the money? Did you get the rest of your inheritance already?"

Yvonne nodded. "It came through this morning. The first thing I did with it was finalize the purchase of this house."

"I thought you had plans for the money. I thought you wanted to invest what was left after you helped Nita."

"I *am* investing it. I'm investing it in us. I also put some of the money aside for when you finish culinary school. It's more than enough for you to start your own bakery."

"My own bakery?"

"That's what you want, isn't it?"

"Yes, but I wasn't serious." Ruby had only started culinary school months ago, having retired from escorting the minute she and Yvonne had made their relationship official. She hadn't even thought about what she wanted to do once she finished. That was too far in the future. "I can't run a bakery. I wouldn't even know how."

"I can help you. I know a thing or two about running a business."

Ruby shook her head. "I couldn't ask you to do that."

"You wouldn't be asking. I'm offering. Like I said, I'm investing in us, in our future together." Yvonne took Ruby's hands in hers. "Speaking of the future, our year is up. We're free of our arrangement. Free of all obligations."

"Yvonne, you couldn't possibly think-"

Yvonne held up her hand. "I don't think you're going to run off on me. But staying together is one thing. Remaining married is another. Marriage is a big commitment, and we've only known each other for a year. If you want us to start over without something that big hanging over us, we can do that. We can stay together, as a couple, and one day get married for real."

Ruby shook her head. "We *are* married for real, Yvonne. And I want us to stay that way. I want to continue to be your wife."

Yvonne smiled. "I'm glad you said that. I want to be your wife too. And I've been thinking about it. The circumstances of our marriage meant we never got to have a real wedding, that dream wedding you always wanted. It's about time we fixed that, don't you think?"

Ruby frowned. "You're not asking me to marry you, are you?"

"I suppose I am." Yvonne took Ruby's left hand and carefully pulled the wedding band from Ruby's finger. "You'll have to forgive me for not getting down on one knee, but we've never cared for doing things the conventional way, have we?"

Ruby's heart skipped a beat. Yvonne was really doing this.

"Ruth Scott." Yvonne held the ring up between them. "My Ruby. Will you marry me?"

Ruby smiled. "Yes, Yvonne. The answer is yes."

Yvonne took Ruby's hand and slid the ring back onto Ruby's finger, then drew her into a deep, endless kiss.

ABOUT THE AUTHOR

Anna Stone is the bestselling author of Being Hers. Her sizzling romance novels, featuring strong, complex, passionate women who love women, are sure to bring the heat.

Anna is in her 30s and lives on the sunny east coast of Australia. When she isn't writing, she can usually be found relaxing on the beach with a book.

Visit annastoneauthor.com for information on her books and to sign up for her newsletter.

facebook.com/AnnaStoneRomance
twitter.com/AnnaStoneAuthor

Printed in Great Britain
by Amazon